LOVING ALL OF ME

BOOK 1 OF THE SPICE SERIES

NALEIGHNA KAI
STEPHANIE M. FREEMAN

MACRO PUBLISHING GROUP

Macro Publishing Group

Macro Marketing & Promotions Group

Loving All of Me © 2023 by Naleighna Kai and Stephanie M. Freeman

Cover designed by: Woodson Creative Studio

Interior design by: Macro Marketing & Promotions Group

Ebook ISBN: 978-1-952871-49-8

ACKNOWLEDGMENTS

Special thanks goes out to: The Creator from whom all Blessings and opportunities flow, Sandy (my true mother), my son, J. L. Woodson (for the awesome cover designs for this Merry Hearts series), Sesvalah, Bettye Odom, Janice M. Allen, Debra J. Mitchell, Royce Slade Morton, Bunny Ervin, J. L. Campbell, Kelly Peterson, Janine A. Ingram, Ehryck F. Gilmore, Betty Clawson, Jamyi Joy, Stephanie M. Freeman, Unique Hiram, Marie L. McKenzie, Shawn Williams, Dr. Vanessa Howard, the Kings of the Castle Ambassadors, Members of Naleighna Kai's Literary Cafe, the members of NK's Tribe Called Success, the members of Namakir Tribe, and to you, my dear readers . . . thank you all for your support.

Much love, peace, and joy,
Naleighna Kai

Stephanie's Acknowledgments:

Naleighna Kai, In a sea or letters and voices, thank you for finding this 'Wordsmith'. and making me part of the tribe. J.L Woodson, what marvelous graphic designer eyes you have. You are the only one that I will ever trust with my covers. Debra Mitchell for her amazing Beta Reader eyes. NK Tribe Called Success you have my heart.

Thanks

Steph-Steph

CHAPTER 1

Something about him sent a delicious shiver of anticipation up Joy's spine. That shiver did a little curtsy at the base of her neck, before sliding down and sending a tingle between her thighs. Her lips parted of their own accord as if to speak, but no sound would come. The Welcome Circle, where all the rules were laid out for the total strangers embarking on an unforgettable journey, had already started.

"Rule one … pajamas stay on the whole time," the flaxen-haired host said.

Desperate. The one word centered in Joy's mind followed by a few more. *How desperate did a woman have to be to attend an event simply to experience someone else's non-sexual touch?* She was here, wasn't she? Settled on a sofa in a room filled with people who had come for one purpose—a Cuddle Party, the new wave of safe adult interaction. Everyone played by the same set of rules. The word "no" was met with a comforting phrase, "Thank you for taking care of yourself."

Joy, a single of mother of two, had held onto the article from the *Chicago Red Eye* for nearly a year before deciding to give it a try.

The gentleman had caught Joy's attention as he swept into the room. He removed a large bottle of Southern Comfort from a brown

1

paper bag and set it on the counter as he settled into a spot near the front door. With his back against the wall, he observed the people spread out in several open rooms. The man was stunningly handsome, with piercing brown eyes, and dark silky hair with a small shock of silver right at the widow's peak. His olive skin had been kissed by the sun, and lips that were the most delectable she'd ever laid eyes on. He wore silk, navy-blue pajamas that complimented his tall, muscular physique. She, along with several others, couldn't help but stare.

"Rule two," their host continued. "You don't have to cuddle with anyone at a cuddle party. Ever."

Oddly enough, Joy expected a place filled with outcasts, people who might have been easily overlooked on the dating scene and everywhere else. Not so. Each man was more handsome than the last. The women were either drop-dead gorgeous or girl-next-door beautiful.

The mysterious stranger remained near the door until it was his turn to share his expectations of the event. The panther-like gait commanded everyone's attention as he sauntered to the center of the living room where everyone was assembled.

"My name is Ali Khan," the smooth, baritone sound beckoned Joy from her thoughts. His voice was as sultry as his appearance, and that was saying something.

The moment his intense gaze met hers, any misgivings she'd felt about being there quickly dissipated.

"I'm here because I love the concept, and the rules. There's a freedom here that's sorely lacking in the world."

As more guests finished their introductions, Joy found that a surprising number of women shared one common thread—molestation, childhood abuse, sexual harassment. Their willingness to share something so personal gave Joy the strength she needed to let her guard down—but only a little.

She glanced at Ali again. One of the rules drifted into the forefront of her mind. *If you mean yes, say "Yes." If you mean no, say "No." If you mean "Maybe," say no. You can always change your mind later.*

Without warning, Ali turned his head and stared at Joy. They were connected across the expanse of the room for several seconds before she broke contact and lowered her eyes. Her pulse raced as if she'd run a marathon mile at top speed, and everything within Joy screamed that if asked, she'd give this man an absolute, "Hell yes."

CHAPTER 2

*S*he is stunning.

Ali was addicted to pleasure. Nothing satisfied him more than giving a woman the ultimate release, and that was second to the kind that happened between her thighs.

One word described the elegant beauty settled—somewhat uncomfortably—on the sofa. Captivating. The women here, including Joy, were hardly the rejects and low-hanging fruit his sons had warned him about. She had a shapely body hidden underneath a long-sleeve, button-down pajama top with matching pants. The color reminded him of mauve sorbet, and it complimented her honey skin. Her raven hair hung in loose curls way past her shoulders. Next, Ali focused on her heart-shaped face with full, perfectly kissable lips and expressive, dark eyes that beckoned to him like a trainer waving a steak in front of a hungry lion.

"My name is Joy," she said. The silky timbre of her voice caused several men in the room to shift slightly. He was no exception. "It's taken me an entire year to show up." She lowered her gaze to the pallet positioned on the floor in the center of the room. "And, I'm glad I'm here."

Joy. The quiet beauty and fluid strength were mere enhancements to her appeal. Her eyes were luminous chocolate orbs that held no secrets. She was like an open book to him. He saw the wariness there, then in a flash it was replaced with a glimpse of certainty, followed by an indicator of acceptance. For him? That thought caused a genuine smile to curl on his lips.

Ali welcomed the idea that the rules left no room for doubt. "Maybe" would be voiced as a "No." No quipping, no explanations, no arguments, no persuasion—a simple "No" and the participant moved on with a simple confirming statement. True power lay in the person that respected the other's boundaries. One look at Joy and he became aware that boundaries and walls were relative. He wasn't sure what led him to come this day, but he was glad he'd followed through.

"I'm not sure what to expect ..." He'd heard her say. Neither did he, but the possibilities had become very intriguing.

Ali remained distant, listening to everyone's story. Some with his eyes closed and his heart open. Last year, this approach had garnered a woman whom he had loved and lost. She'd shared a life story filled with such tragedy that his heart hurt every time he thought about what she'd been through. He'd longed to protect her, but through no fault of his own, he had lost her. Family obligation had caused Reign to break his heart. Not because she wanted to, but because she had no choice. He knew all about familial ties. Thankfully, he was on the flip-side of that heartbreak. He wished Reign well and now rejoiced in new possibilities.

Wounded. Betrayed. Strong.

So many vibrations swirled about that woman across the room, but he zeroed in on the two that mattered most. *Survivor. Resilient.*

Those two he could identify with. They echoed in his own life. Ali had never realized he had a "savior complex" until now. Joy had an exotic beauty, and elegance even through the pain that was so clearly etched in her velvet brown eyes. It gave him an overwhelming urge to see her smile.

He thought back to his ready-made life with the built-in wife. Happiness was a constant stranger during that time, thanks to his father. Though he'd understood his father's need to be welcomed back into the family fold, it did little to assuage the bitterness Ali felt at being served up as a physical sacrifice. He'd never wanted the marriage he'd been forced into, nor the burden of carrying his father's penance when he'd married a woman outside of their culture. The sins of the father had indeed been visited on the son.

Ali was a self-made millionaire who had fulfilled all his family's expectations—marriage to a woman from an East Indian family, financial stability, and four children to carry on the Khan name. But that was over. He had no intention of spending the rest of his life in a mediocre marriage he'd never asked for when so many possibilities awaited him. He gained the ire of his father and in-laws when he divorced Sonali, but he had assured them that she would always be financially secure. His duty was done.

Not one for loose ends, in business or his personal life, he had eased Sonali into living a life without him and had no objection when she had run into the arms of the childhood friend.

Now the time had come for Ali to pursue his own happiness, and he had every intention of doing just that.

Dwelling on the past was useless, so he refocused his energy on Joy. No point in trying to hide it. She was the only one he wanted to encounter that night. His mind drifted to thoughts of her lush, sensuous body relaxed in mild supplication, as though the art of seduction seeped from her pores. Her demeanor softened when he introduced himself. That acceptance resonated all over her body as she said the word he'd longed to hear drip from her lips—Yes.

Ali knew then and there—Joy would be his.

Completely.

CHAPTER 3

"Ali," he said, both snatching her attention away from one of the hosts and startling her at the same time. Joy watched people dispersed into couples and groups, but somehow, she'd been oblivious to Ali moving across the room. Now he was mere inches away.

She blinked, trying to clear her thoughts, and inhaled the clean, cool scent of him. So many sensations swirled about Ali that she had a hard time choosing one to hold on to.

"Joy," she replied, extending her hand to him.

"Permission to touch you?"

She hesitated. Oh, shoot. She'd forgotten already. *Rule ... you must ask permission and receive a verbal "Yes" before you touch anyone.*

Complying with the rules meant that every touch, no matter how small, required consent. Permission to touch a hand did not mean the same permission was given to touch an arm.

"Yes," she said in a breathy whisper. "You may touch me."

Ali moved in a little closer. Slowly, he took her small hand in his. Joy noticed the size difference as he stroked a single fingertip across her palm. A strong need hummed within her. It had been suppressed so long that she barely realized the feeling of wanting to be connected to someone. Thanks to her family, Joy was desensitized to any real emotion; starting from the time she'd been forced to leave home at twelve to find a safe place to live.

Don't dwell on the past. Only the now.

Ali moved forward, keeping her hand securely in his. He guided her to the space she'd vacated on the sofa. All around them people claimed chairs, loveseats, mattresses draped in crisp sheets, and comfy-looking pallets on the floor. Guests had also gathered around the kitchen island, holding animated conversations as they sampled an array of food and tempting sweets. The atmosphere was relaxed, but still rife with anticipation.

People of all ethnic groups, backgrounds, and genders were represented, each wanting one thing—to connect. It wasn't surprising that some chose to stave their hunger with food while striking up a conversation before being drawn into any physical contact.

Ali moved closer to Joy. "May I hold you?"

"Yes, you may."

Joy was sitting next to Ali but shifted so that she was now curled into him. The feel of his chest against her face, the muscles that rippled underneath, paled by comparison to his arms securing her in an embrace so wonderful that she did something she never thought possible. Joy let her guard so far down that she suddenly blurted out, "Why are you here?" Only to be floored by his answer.

"I came … for you."

A jolt of electricity ricocheted through her entire body at his words. Closing her eyes, Joy allowed the safety of his arms to work their magic. The memories she'd held at bay resurfaced, possibly because she was in the safest place possible to relive them. The energy he exuded was that of a man who was strong, powerful, secure in who he was and his place in the world.

I came … for you.

Those words. He couldn't know what a balm they were to her soul. No one, not her mother, nor her father had ever made her feel this secure. This safe. Not even the family who delighted in treating her like an outcast because she'd refused to follow her mother and sisters into the family business of prostitution. No one had ever come for her. Ever.

* * *

AN HOUR LATER, the event ended. Reluctantly, Ali stood and helped Joy to her feet.

"I can't tell you the last time I enjoyed an evening so thoroughly."

A huge smile overtook Joy's face. "Me either. I'm so glad I came."

Her happiness mirrored his own. "That makes two of us."

"May I walk you back to your car?"

"Oh, you don't have to," she said dismissively.

"I know, but I'd like to."

A tremor of excitement rippled through her body. "Of course."

Ali placed his hand at the small of Joy's back, and they moved around the room saying their goodbyes and encountered a few genuine smiles, and some that were noticeably forced. It didn't make one bit of difference to Ali.

A touch of humidity caressed them as they left the house. Ali slipped his arm fully around Joy's waist and maneuvered her to the inside as they walked.

"This is me," she said as they reached a silver Buick Encore. She pressed the fob to unlock the door. She slipped inside, turned the car on and lowered the window. "Thank you for an amazing evening."

Ali lowered himself so that he filled the window space. "It was my pleasure. I also had an evening I won't soon forget."

Mesmerized, Joy confessed. "I'm having a hard time leaving because it means I'll never see you again."

He smiled. "There's another Cuddle Party in a week. Meet me there?"

"I'll be there," she promised.

A second later, he released her hand. He gazed into her eyes a final time before he said, "Goodnight, Joy. Be safe and sleep well."

"You too, Ali," she replied.

As Joy pulled away, she glanced at the rearview mirror. He was still standing where she left him.

<h1 style="text-align:center">CHAPTER 4</h1>

*J*oy found it incredible that one chance meeting could change a person's life so thoroughly, but then again, she was no stranger to having plans upset by unforeseen circumstances beyond one's control.

When other twelve-year-olds were enjoying their lives, she was running for hers. Joy had been forced to strike out on her own, and she never looked back.

A red brick building with a sign—CLEANING WOMAN WANTED. INQUIRE INSIDE got her attention.

Carrying her meager belongings, she went inside.

A balding, brown-skinned barrel of a man took one look at Joy and said, "I don't want no trouble here."

"And I didn't bring any," she shot back, following him into the first-floor apartment that served as a makeshift office.

She paused, processing her next words carefully. "I won't make it where I live now if I don't protect myself."

"From who?"

"My mother. Her men. All of them."

Earnest and his wife, Donna, had taken her in and set her up in their smallest apartment.

Soon, everyone in the building became her new family. She learned more from the tenants than she'd ever learned with her relatives. Already a survivor, she learned patience and planning, acceptance of all lifestyles, financial responsibility, and how to be a positive member of society. Along with how to play Bid Whist and Chess.

Unfortunately, nothing could have prepared Joy for the return of someone she never wanted to see again. At eighteen, Joy had achieved a 4.0 grade point average and was valedictorian, but instead of going to Howard to enjoy a full ride, her world came crashing down about her ears.

Ella, Joy's mother, arrived on her doorstep with a newborn baby in tow.

"Your sister's still hyped up on them drugs," Ella said, without so much as a hello. Her voice was raspy from years of chain-smoking. She shifted the baby in her arms so Joy could get a good look. "The State's threatening to put her boy in the system. We can't have that."

A sense of foreboding signaled that this visit would not end happily—at least not for Joy.

"Well, I'm leaving for D.C. in three days," Joy said, frowning that her mother had such a lax hold on the baby. "So, I won't be able to babysit for you."

"I ain't say nothin' about no babysittin'." Ella moved the baby to her other arm. "Naw, you're gonna keep this little bastard until Ebbie gets outta rehab."

"No, I won't," Joy protested, placing another blouse into the suitcase. "I have a life. I have school."

Ella shrugged. "Gonna have to put that off for a minute. Family's more important."

Joy straightened her back, glaring at her mother. "Since when? When did family see my importance? I busted my ass to finish grammar school, then to get through high school. Family didn't have a damn thing to do with that."

"You didn't have to leave," Ella said, averting her gaze. "That was Willis who tried that mess with you, and he moved out."

"Didn't keep those others from trying," Joy countered. "Damn shame I had to sleep with a knife under my pillow to keep them off me."

Ella seemed more frustrated now that the baby was struggling and crying, almost as if he knew he wasn't safe in her arms. "College is a waste of good money," she snapped while scanning the apartment with disdain. "Yep, a waste."

"It's not your money," Joy retorted, wondering why the hospital band was still on the child's tiny wrist. "And you're not footing the bill for anything, so your thoughts don't matter." Joy continued to pack.

"This baby needs you. Just a month."

"I can't help you."

"Two weeks," she countered. "Big Sal and I got things to do."

"Like what. Pimp out someone else?"

"Why you gotta be so ugly," Ella snarled, placing the baby on the sofa and backing away. "I bought some pampers and milk and stuff. They right outside. I'll bring some money. It's only for a few days. She'll get out by then."

Joy picked up the baby and curled him in her arms, and he smiled up at her as he calmed down.

"It won't be long," Ella replied. "See, he's lovin' you already." With that, her mother bolted out the door.

Those "two weeks" in rehab were followed by months of unkept promises. Joy had to get a job to support herself and the child. She had prayed that she could eventually take her place among the next group of incoming freshman.

That was one prayer that God didn't answer.

Not even a year later, Ella showed up and managed to drop off yet another of Ebbie's children—a girl child this time. College and the life Joy had planned all but circled the bowl and went down in a royal flush.

Now, fourteen years had passed. Joy had made something of herself. With no help from her dysfunctional family, she had graduated from college with a Bachelor of Science degree, and with honors. She had landed a coveted job at the Drug Enforcement Agency as a Forensic Chemist, and an agent. A few weeks ago, she had been promoted to a special task force that was assigned to bust a man, Adesh Kholi, suspected in an illegal drug and sex trafficking operation. A big break for her, and she vowed to do whatever it took to nail his butt to the proverbial wall.

CHAPTER 5

Over the next few weeks, Ali attended several cuddle parties hoping to lay eyes on Joy, but she hadn't returned. He always left early, disappointed at her absence. He couldn't stop thinking about her and wondered what would make her stay away.

Now he was at yet another one. Surprisingly, not an ounce of sexual tension permeated the event. Each member of the group seemed absorbed by the person they were near. Some were checking the lay of the land by connecting with conversation before being drawn into any physical contact.

A woman with ivory skin and platinum hair had her head cradled in the lap of a buxom Black woman whose caress was so powerful that the blonde, who had come with her husband, could hardly keep her eyes open while absorbing the simple pleasures of the stranger's touch.

Others lay on one of the larger pallets in a formation considered a classic "puppy pile," groups of people spooning—one person in front, another in back—with the result resembling a human pinwheel.

None of it appealed to him.

Moments later, a woman sidled up to him, asking in a husky voice,

"You're looking for her, aren't you? You're not going to come out and play with anyone else?"

Ali gave her a patient smile. "She suits me just fine. Thank you."

Waves of disappointment rolled off her, and the same would hold true of the other women when he politely declined each time they asked for some sort of touch. He wanted Joy. Only Joy.

One of them, emboldened, sought to take another approach.

Ali tensed, and quickly adjusted so he was out of the woman's reach. "No."

The blonde froze and allowed her hand to drop by her side. "You're supposed to mingle," she said in a tone that held a mild reproach.

"No, I'm supposed to do what I damn well please," he countered, smiling to take the edge off. "And right now, she pleases me. Immensely."

Ali spent a half hour deflecting other requests before people got the message that he should be left alone.

Even Callie, one of the hosts, ventured over at one point to put her bid in to separate Ali from the notion that only Joy could command his interest, probably because some of the others had mentioned their discontent.

"Either this—the rules—are going to be followed to the letter," he said. "Or you all have been giving lip service."

Callie inched back, sweeping a gaze over several women who stood off to the side, watching the exchange before she said, "You're right. It's just that she's new and the old-timers are feeling a little put out that you've chosen to be so insular again." She glanced at Ali. "Are you a couple or something?"

Rule: Respect your relationship agreements and communicate with your partner.

"Never met her before that day," he admitted.

"Wow," Callie said, perching at the edge of the sofa. "And y'all have connected on this level already?"

"Despite this event being about non-sexual touch, people have met their significant others here, right? It's not unusual for something deeper to transpire at some point. Is it?"

"Okay then," she said getting to her feet, rubbing her hand down the front of her flannel pajamas. "Well, enjoy yourself."

"I will. Thank you."

"You really are handsome," she said, and this time there was a bit of seduction in her tone.

"I get that a lot," he replied. "She's the one woman who didn't say anything of the sort." His gaze reconnected with Callie whose stiff shoulders showed her displeasure. "Just think of how refreshing that is for someone to see past the physical and simply allow a man to ... be."

Callie whipped out her cell, slid the screen to her social media account and turned the screen to face him. Joy's image greeted him, along with her last name. She had changed her hair a little, added some blonde highlights, but those dark brown eyes with that hint of sadness, were still the same.

Ali smiled, saying, "Thank you. Enjoy the party."

He called a private investigator on his way home.

* * *

JOY WHISKED past her assistant's desk and into her office. A bouquet of flowers waited on her desk. She slid open the note and read the perfectly even script that said,

"Joy, I request the honor of your presence for one day. One day to prove that our first meeting should not have been a one-time experience. One day for me to make you smile. Give me a call if you're a "Yes" or even a "Maybe."

Joy flipped the card, studying it for several moments, surprised that he found her. Flowers—all orchids. Purple, her favorite color. He really did listen that night. She hadn't been able to get him off her mind. So much so that she pictured him before she closed her eyes at night. Imagined the feel of him beside her, those arms around her.

She stayed away from the parties because she didn't understand if his intentions were real, or if he simply wanted to get her in his bed.

16

Ali Khan was a mega-rich, handsome bachelor, who was probably used to getting what he wanted from women. As a DEA agent, she knew how to take care of herself physically—she studied martial arts, carried a revolver—but her heart was something different. In her line of work, which was dominated by men, none of them had interested her. She was intrigued by Ali because of the way he made her feel that first time they met.

Was it real? Or was this simply a game to him?

CHAPTER 6

*J*oy's expression of child-like elation was one of the most beautiful things he'd ever seen. Her genuine excitement and happiness transformed her entire body. She was brimming with excitement, and practically dragged Ali behind her as they headed to the entrance. True to his word, Ali aimed to bring about that smile by taking her to Indiana Beach Amusement Park on Lake Schaffer. The place was packed with roller coasters, a water park, amusement rides, and arcade games.

They rode each of the six roller coasters several times.

"I didn't know you liked them that much," he laughed, as they stood in line for another ride.

"Me either," she laughed. "My first time."

Ali's head snapped to her. "You've never been on a roller coaster?"

"I've never been to an amusement park." She shook her head in awe. "And I can't tell you how much fun I'm having."

Ali was still trying to process Joy's words. He hadn't considered this possibility. He'd wanted to take her there to lighten her mood and make her smile. He tried not to ruin the moment by showing how that sad bit of news broke his heart. Instead, he wrapped her in his arms and said, "Okay, after this, what next?"

"Well, next I'm going to kick your ass at the shooting gallery," she bragged. "I'm an expert shot."

"Oh really?" he countered. "Well, so am I. Sounds like a challenge has just been issued."

* * *

AN HOUR LATER, Ali and Joy headed back to the car. Joy was carrying a big teddy bear. Both had won more stuffed animals from their shooting contests, but the storage space in his sports car didn't allow for them.

"Next time, I'll drive the SUV," he said as they gave away another animal to the parents of a child passing by

"I'm glad we were able to give them to kids. Besides," she added snuggling her bear. "I get to keep this fella right here."

"I'm glad you enjoyed yourself." He concentrated on merging onto the ramp to head home. "You don't know how happy it makes me to see you smile."

She'd had a journalist friend, Nia Tate check him out. She prayed she wasn't mistaken about his character. Though they hadn't known each other long, her heart swelled just thinking about how much she already cared for him.

The need to reciprocate his kindness was strong. Staring out the window instead of at him gave her the strength to speak her truth, she told him about her past. Ali remained absolutely silent. The only way she knew what he was feeling was by the occasional grip on his steering wheel that was so tight, his knuckles turned white.

"Despite my family's attempts at sabotage, I finally went to college," she told him. "I got my undergraduate degree in Chemistry and became a Forensic Chemist. I work for the Drug Enforcement Agency."

"You work for the DEA?" he said in awe. "Impressive. What exactly do you do?"

"I'm an agent, but I work in a lab," she answered. "I analyze unidentified substances so that they might be used to detect new narcotics flowing into our cities. The new compounds I examine help determine the processes and materials that were used to manufacture them and the effects on the physiology of the users. I'm also called on to provide expert testimony for legal proceedings, and to assist in investigations."

"So, you're trying to stay one step ahead of the bad guys that are out there making this stuff, and the ones selling it," he concluded, easing onto the ramp for a connecting interstate.

"Yes. While the criminals are racing to produce drugs that are more powerful, undetectable, and addict people faster, we're working to produce better detection methods and treatment systems."

"I can tell you're very passionate about your job."

"I am," Joy replied. "Working to get the bad guys destroying families off the street is important to me. But it's not just that. I'm on a task force to help stop sex traffickers that are using these illegal substances to subdue and hook their captives."

Given her background, the subject hit very close to home. Quickly, she turned to observe him. Looking for something. Any kind of discomfort that would tell her what she needed to know.

Nothing.

When he noticed her watching him, he reached out and took her hand. He brought it to his lips. "Sweetheart, if only you could see what I see in you. You've overcome so much heartache, and more adversity than should be allowed. And yet here you are. Following your dream to rid the city of drugs, and living a decent, stand-up life. You could've succumbed to your family's pressure, and yet you didn't. That takes guts, Joy. Pure determination to survive no matter the odds. You, my love, are way stronger than you give yourself credit for."

Something in his tone broke down another layer of the ice encasing her heart. A rush of emotions swept through her.

She realized two things—she was falling so deep for Ali Khan, and that was going to wreak havoc in her life.

CHAPTER 7

"*I*'m a self-made man," he said on the interstate heading toward Chicago. "I have several companies, but I got my first break by tapping into one of the least serviced industries. Snake venom."

Joy's eyebrows rose. "Really?"

He nodded. "My business took off. I was in high demand, and the fact that procuring the serum was such a deadly process meant that we commanded top dollar. When hospitals called because someone's life hung in the balance we were there. Eventually, the need for rare medicines that only a few pharmaceuticals manufactured meant people wanted to avoid going through government red tape."

Joy nodded. "Trust me; I understand slow bureaucratic processes."

"I can imagine," he said. "We didn't have to worry about the number of years for research and development, lawsuits from patients who experienced the ill effects when companies didn't develop medications properly before rushing them to market." He steered the car into the fast lane and picked up speed. "On the flipside, my export management company was also lucrative because it solely handled U.S. medicines and pharmaceuticals, managed the details of hiring distributors, developing marketing materials and preparing shipping logistics. From there, we had the capital we needed to invest in IPOs and real estate ventures."

"Do you still run it? The pharmaceutical company?"

He shook his head. "My son, Adesh handles everything. I'm pretty hands off with the day-to-day activities. Frees me up to pursue other, more pleasurable experiences."

Joy laced her hands and placed them on her lap. "That's a lot of responsibility for someone so young, isn't it? How old is he, about twenty-five?"

Ali laughed. "Even younger. He's twenty-three. But he was at the top of his class and excelled at everything he's put his mind to. I'm extremely proud of his hard work and accomplishments."

She pondered that for a moment. "Are any more of your children in the family businesses?"

"All of them. My next oldest is Nikhil. He's twenty-two. And then my daughter, Vanya, is twenty, and Kyra eighteen. All of them started working at the ground level and will build from there. Nikhil, Kyra, and Vanya are still interns, working around their school schedules. It's important that they don't take anything for granted. I want them to learn to work hard, treat the staff well and not to take for granted that because their last name is Khan, it entitles them to get ahead without putting in the work."

"That's a great work ethic," Joy said. "Did you learn that from your parents?"

His expression hardened momentarily. "For the most part, but we weren't born with means. I acquired them later," he told her. "Business is my passion. Being a success was drummed into me since I was a child," he said in a matter-of-fact tone. "As was the importance of family."

Joy offered a comforting hand to hold. Ali squeezed it and continued, glancing over at Joy.

"More than anything, I understand the need to put family first. I listened to your story, and I know you're aware of what that means."

Ali brought her hand to his lips, kissing the underside of her wrist, then dropped a bombshell. "Come away with me. Let's go on that vacation you always dreamed of."

CHAPTER 8

Two weeks after that conversation, Joy froze at the base of the stairs as her daughter, Lyric, rebelled against the plans Joy had arranged.

"Why can't we go? We're not babies," Lyric said blowing off staying the weekend with Donna and Ernie, who had been grandparents for them from the moment Joy took them in.

"I want to know who my real mother is. We've got aunts and uncles and cousins and stuff that we don't know because you've been keeping us away from them."

Joy almost couldn't breathe. She'd been her niece's mother for thirteen years of her life. Now because Ebbie and Ella had made a concerted effort to get the children back, they had finally succeeded in disrupting her household. And she knew why. Ella wanted revenge.

Ella showed up, unexpected again, attempting to drop off yet a third child that Joy's sister conceived and gave birth to while in the throes of addiction.

"No," Joy said, this time fully blocking the entrance, so her mother couldn't slither in like last time. "I can't take another one."

"You doin' good with them," Ella said, inching forward. "They healthy. They seem happy, too. So, what's one more?"

"I'm paying up the ying-yang for childcare and medical bills because

they have issues, thanks to their mother's selfishness. But that's all right,"
she said to Ella. "I'm going to social services to apply for some
assistance."

Ella nearly dropped the child in her arms; her eyes widened to the size of
saucers. "No. No. No. Don't do that." She shook her head vigorously, jowls
flapping with the movement. "No. No. Don't do nothing like that. I'll give
you the money."

Joy scoffed, inching forward. "I don't want to depend on you for anything
—ever again."

"You selfish little bitch," Ella snarled

"Selfish?" Joy almost lost her balance. "Oh, that's rich coming from a
woman who put those bastards warming her bed above the welfare of her
own children. Rich from a woman who keeps pulling her daughter out of
rehab because she's her best money-maker." Joy moved forward, so Ella was
fully in the hallway.

"Leave," Joy said through her teeth. "I don't want to see you or any of my
so-called family again."

And she didn't. Not until the day she learned how deep Ella's deception
had gone.

Everything came to a head the day the social worker, Terri
Rayford, came by to check out the new house Joy had purchased and
to finish the applications for several services for which Joy had
applied.

Joy rocked Lyric in her arms while keeping an eye on Ms. Rayford who
said, "So you're looking to have permanent custody of Jason and Lyric."

"I've been the only one caring for them since they came home from the
hospital." Joy tucked a blanket around Lyric.

The woman observed as Joy reached into the top file drawer of a cabinet
in her make-shift study area, then extracted several sets of manila folders.
She passed them to Ms. Rayford who took her time perusing the documents,
frowning with each turn of the page.

Finally, Ms. Rayford said, "I don't understand any of this. Your mother's
been receiving both financial and medical benefits for the children since they
came home from the hospital."

All the air left Joy's body. "Wait ... what? What?" She shook her head.

"No, that can't be right. I've come out of my own pocket for their medical care and for everything. I love them."

"And I can tell," Ms. Rayford said with a smile. "This whole place speaks to how much you care." She tapped the edges of the documents and slid them back into the folders. "I need copies of these. Your mother has committed fraud. She might end up facing charges."

Joy absorbed that bit of news. "My mother has never cared about me," Joy said. "She let me work damn near to the bone to take care of them. All while she pocketed that money and didn't even tell me about the medical cards because she wanted to hold to her lie." Joy nodded, her decision made. "Yes, I want full custody of Jason and Lyric. And I want the truth to come out. If my mother ends up in jail, then that's exactly what she deserves."

Defrauding the government. Uncle Sam did not play about his coins.

Neither did Joy Cullins.

AND NOW, years later, Lyric wanted to walk straight into the lion's den, and nothing Joy could say seemed to sway her.

CHAPTER 9

$\mathcal{J}$oy, still reeling from Lyric's rant, focused her gaze on her son who said. "Don't look this way. This don't have nothing to do with me. You're my mama all day long." He focused on his sister. "She threw us away."

Lyric's head snapped up. "You don't know that."

"People know all about her. Her next high was more important than us," Jason reasoned "I can't forget that. Ella—that's grandma's name, right?"

Joy nodded, trying to keep her emotions at bay.

"She's been coming around here, filling your head with crazy stuff. I thought you were smarter than that."

Lyric lowered her gaze to the carpet.

Jason gestured to Joy. "This woman right here has been everything, and you're going to kick her to the curb for someone who just showed up. You are all kinds of stupid."

Lyric pointed at Joy, screaming, "She let our other brothers and sisters go into foster care. We don't know who they are, or where they are."

Joy had had enough. "I was eighteen," she shot back, her hands balled into tight fists. "I had you, and I had Jason. That was all I could handle. I was just coming out of being a child myself. The only people who helped were people at Garfield Building. *That's* our family." She shook her head, angry to be having this discussion long before she'd prepared to have it. "There came a time when I had to say no. She had nine other children. If I kept just one more, you wouldn't have the life you do now. We had to survive. And that meant me having to make some hard choices."

Lyric plopped down on the sofa, pouting.

"Let's talk about what this is really about," Joy said, moving until she stood directly in front of her daughter. "You're mad right now because I won't let you see that boy, and they're saying you can? Am I supposed to just let you do anything you want? Like you're the adult around here? When you're slacking on your schoolwork and chores? Let's talk about that."

Lyric huffed and jumped to her feet. "Nah, you're just mad I want to live with my real mother. She didn't give us up," she said, shifting her focus to Jason. "Grandma said she stole us."

The teenager really knew how to put the dagger in and twisted it at every turn. "You know what? I'm not going to fight a battle you don't want me to win."

Ella's efforts were working against Joy, so much so that Lyric didn't engage in normal conversations anymore; just demands and arguments. "I can't keep you from learning this lesson, and no, I'm not mad or anything like that. I'm disappointed, but I'm not mad."

Same way Joy had wanted to shake some sense into Ebbie before she gave birth to Champagne, Champale, Martell, Alize, Porsche, Mercedes, Lexus, Irish Rose, and Morticia. Glad she stopped having children at that point because the next in line was Pugsley or Lurch—or worse, Ripple, after that old school brand of liquor. Thankfully, she'd been in the movie phase of her life when she named Jason and Lyric. There were nine other children out there. Joy had to wonder why her mother and sister were so keen on getting their hands on Lyric.

"I can't be with you every minute of the day," Joy conceded. "I can say whatever, but you've already been sneaking over there. At some point, you'll find out the reason I was trying to get the hell up out of there. I hope you don't, but I know my people." She spread out her hands. "Oh, they won't make you go to school. They'll let you run with the boys. No curfew. Sounds good, right?" Joy lowered to her knees until she was eye level with Lyric. "Trust me; it's going to cost you something. You just don't know what it is yet."

Joy inhaled and released a long, slow breath. She desperately needed to process this whole conversation in a way that didn't unnecessarily burden her children. Standing, she headed for the privacy of the upstairs, but a glance over her shoulder at Lyric crestfallen expression almost made her waver. But then the teen quickly schooled her features into a mask of resolve, lifted her chin, and whipped out her cell to send a text.

Joy walked over to her daughter, kissed her forehead that was peppered with a thin layer of perspiration. She made it up the stairs but froze at the top landing when Jason said, "I've been there. That house smells like ass and devastation. We have a good life here, much better than our brothers and sisters ever had, and you're letting some boy get all up in your head."

"You don't know nothing."

"Really? He was with Vee last night and Celia the week before that. As soon as he gets what he wants from you, he'll be onto the next one."

CHAPTER 10

$\mathcal{J}$ason had practically dragged Lyric out of the house so they could make it to Donna and Ernie's spot, leaving Joy to go on a date with Ali.

Two months had passed since she'd laid eyes on him. A dynamic, rich, handsome businessman was showing intense interest in Joy, and she didn't know what to make of it. What did they have in common? Why was he so intent on having her in his life? She would love to run away with him for the weekend he'd been asking for—be impulsive for a change instead of always doing what was expected of her. With her job and the fact that his line of work was diametrically opposed, she wasn't sure. Would he understand the reason she was a mother figure to children who might not take it so well that she finally had an interest in having an intimate relationship? How had she gone from a woman with no options to a woman who had the best option in the world—one that complicated her already chaotic life?

Ali purchased tickets for the Lion King with a late dinner to follow at the Grand Lux Cafe. He offered to pick her up from her place in Hyde Park, and to her surprise, she agreed.

"Hey, beautiful."

"Hey, yourself handsome," Joy replied before stepping aside to let

Ali enter her three-story classic Victorian home on a picturesque street.

The graystone, built in 1903, had been a fixer-upper, but Donna and Ernie had called in a few favors and convinced the construction team working on their new apartment building down the street to renovate Joy's home for a significantly lower price. Now her Garfield family lived near her in the historic district of Hyde Park.

The place boasted high ceilings, original hardwood floors, woodwork, and two fireplaces, oak wainscoting walls, and the original ornamental beam ceilings in the dining room. To Joy's delight, the place also had pocket doors and a parlor, along with a few modern upgrades that added to its vintage charm.

"What's the matter?" Ali asked.

"It's nothing," she said quickly. "Just an argument with my daughter. She didn't want to go to her grandparent's house this weekend."

"Donna and Ernie?"

She nodded. "She wants to go over my sister's house. I don't want to push Lyric away, but I also don't want to condone her setting herself up for heartache. That's a slippery slope I'd rather my children not have to walk. I've taught them how to protect themselves—and even prepared them in the instance that someone tries to get to me by using them. They know the normal non-verbal cues to look for in a rescue. But I can't seem to rescue Lyric from when it comes to this."

"I understand. You just have to do what you can without coming flat out and forbidding her to go. That will only push her right into your sister's arms."

"Over my dead body," Joy said, seriously.

"I hope not, I happen to really enjoy looking at this body." Ali leaned in and kissed the nape of her neck. "This part." Next, his hand roamed down her back and connected across her full hips. He squeezed the firm flesh before sliding his hand to rest at the small of her back. After a lingering kiss that was filled with promise, he found a sensitive spot right next to her earlobe. Giving it his undivided attention, Ali lined a trail of kisses down her neck. "And this."

Before Joy could utter a sound, he had picked her up and settled her firmly against the wall. Molded against him, Joy wrapped her arms around his neck.

"Did you say the children were gone?" he asked huskily.

"They're already at Donna and Ernie's house," she replied with considerable effort.

As if the thought was too tempting, Ali wrenched his mouth away from Joy's and released her. He took a few steps back, but his facial expression still held all the desire coursing through his veins. "I'm sorry. I got a bit carried away."

Joy smoothed her hair back over her shoulders. "We both did."

"Sometimes," Ali said, peering at her, "It's almost as though you've never been in love before."

Joy averted her gaze.

"Joy?"

"I never … I never wanted to bring a man in my life," she confessed. "Bring them in my house to have any control over my children. Too much can happen. And I didn't want to hurt some man because I'd always be looking for him to …" she shrugged. "So, no, I've never been in love." She focused those velvet brown orbs on him. "Never wanted to screw up someone else because every touch would be suspect, every look at my children would have me reading something more into it. That wouldn't be fair to him."

Ali remained silent, not sure what to say to that. Her logic was sound, but the choice to not have at least one intimate experience was something he couldn't fathom.

"And before you get your hopes up that I'm a virgin or something like that … I'm not. I just can't remember my first time."

Ali shifted, peered at her, sensing a deeper meaning hid behind those words.

"I had to get my medical records. An STD at age five. A treatable one, but still, how did I get it? Ella blamed it on some random man, but given my sister's history, I'm beginning to think it wasn't just one."

The anger he felt far surpassed anything else he could feel.

"That's why I have such a hard time believing that your affection is sincere," Joy said. "How can you, with everything you have, want someone like me?"

Ali pulled her into his arms. "How can I not want you—everything you are, everything that you've been through has made you the most desirable woman in the world. That doesn't have anything to do with what you have, but all about who you are." Ali kissed her gently. "If we're going to go to the theatre, I think we'd better get going."

"I know," she agreed, moving around him to grab her jacket from the arm of the sofa.

"You haven't given me an answer, yet."

Joy frowned. "About what?"

Now it was Ali's turn to grimace. "About going away with me. Or did you forget?"

"I haven't forgotten," she said. "I was going to call you when I got home from work today to discuss it, but then Lyric and I got into it, and it slipped my mind. I've thought about it, and of course, I want to go with you."

Ali grinned and kissed her again. "I'm glad to hear it."

CHAPTER 11

$\mathcal{M}$isery is a disease, and I am the cure.

Saying the words aloud was almost better than the first hit of the most addictive drug. Sure, it wasn't the wisest move to try the product. But with an antidote waiting close by, the temptation was undeniable. After all, Adesh had started off in Quality Assurance at his father's company and now he was destined to do more. He couldn't just sell a product without making sure that it was the best of the best.

And it *was* the best. It was better than a million-dollar dream in a three-dollar crack pipe. Drug Empires from all over the world would kneel before him. Meth would become a myth and marijuana that smelled of skunk or bull urine would fade to memory. Saints, sinners, beggars and kings would crawl to his doorstep, and he would be merciful.

Playing the long game had always been the sole focus. Adesh Kahn would provide salvation with one hand and damnation with the other. He would provide the antidote that reversed the effects of a drug overdose while creating a new drug that was even more addictive than anything out on the black and upper-level markets.

"Papa will never approve of this," Vanya said as she leaned in the doorway to his corner office overlooking the towering landscapes across the north Chicago skyline.

"Papa," Adesh scoffed with a dismissive wave of his hand. "Forgot where he came from. He does not remember the days of eating sand and wishing it was Ambrosia."

"And neither do you," she shot back. "He worked his fingers until they bled, risked his life entering into this business, all to make sure we never knew a day of poverty or had to resort to eating sand to fill our bellies like so many other families back home."

"Living without both parents in the home is poverty," he snapped, and the anger he felt from that experience was nothing he ever tried to hide.

Vanya left her place at the doorway. "You should count yourself lucky that you are not bound to the traditions of our culture." Before taking a seat in one of the chairs in front of his desk, she said. "Our father did not have the luxury of choice in brides. He paid a blood debt to ensure that his mother and father had a future. He made sure that we were all taken care of. Is he not entitled to a sliver of happiness?"

Adesh glanced at the portrait of his father hanging on the wall above the fireplace in the expertly crafted masculine office and frowned. "And he sullies his body on women that are not of our culture," he said with a sigh. "You have a woman's heart and mind." He rounded the desk to kneel before her, placing a comforting hand on her arm. "You are young. There are things you do not understand about life. No matter. When your belly is swollen with child, you will remember your place and leave the heavy thinking to men."

Vanya slapped his hand from her arm and stood. "And with this woman's heart and mind, and Papa's faith in my abilities, I may run this office before you ever will. What happened to you, brother? How did genocide become the task of the day? You've seen what the horrors of addiction can do to a person. Have you forgotten what it did to your fiancé, Shiva? "

"Unlike diabetes, addiction is a choice. No one forced her to put that needle in her arm." The moon bathed every darkened area in

Adesh's office in a stale blue hue that created more shadows than light. "If you tell him, you'll have to admit your part."

"I don't know what you mean," she said while fixing the olive-green pashmina over her shoulder.

"Your intended, of course," he sneered. "Why else would he want a nosy little ingrate like you?" He rearranged the pashmina over her arm and let his eyes crawl up to her face. "As I recall you begged me to help you convince him you two were a good match. How else do you think I did it?"

She shuddered with disgust.

"Tell Papa and you risk losing your one true love. Hold your tongue and I will make sure he becomes your husband."

Vanya stood and walked to the door, giving him her back to ponder. "Don't you mean slave?"

"What's the difference?" he asked as she closed the door. "Come on, my darling sister. What's a little addiction between master and slave?"

CHAPTER 12

$\mathcal{A}$li settled into a chair at the head of the dining room table of his Walton Street condo. Expansive terraces overlooked downtown Lake Michigan while gracious, flowing living spaces, including a master suite and complete spa bath leading to a private pool area right outside of a paneled den, with a home theater and glass-encased wine cellar.

The minute he realized that he desired to have Joy in his life on a permanent basis, and wanted her to meet his children, he felt it wise to gauge their feelings and put an eye on Adesh to see if there were any telling points. He brought them in for a sit-down dinner to have a discussion, so they wouldn't be blindsided by the news that he now had a significant other.

His son Adesh was very much rooted in East Indian culture, and that meant marrying and doing business only with those in a certain circle. He was more like his grandfather than Ali, which saddened him. He'd tried to raise his children to be open, worldly, and compassionate, but his wife's old-fashioned family had been a greater influence.

Diving headfirst into the conversation, Ali was not prepared for their resistance to something that was so vital to his happiness.

"How are you going to choose *another* Black woman over all the eligible Indian and Arabian women in our circle?" Adesh asked, glaring at his father. "Slumming again?"

"Whew, look at the time," his oldest daughter, Vanya said. "That's my cue. I'm going back to work before there's bloodshed."

"Careful," Ali warned his son as Vanya swept out of the house. "Choose your words wisely.

"If you must date them, why not find the ones with money?" Nikhil chimed in, while pulling a glass figurine from the shelf.

"Nikhil, Joy is doing well for herself, and her children," he countered.

"Children?" Vanya said, her excitement warming him. "How many and how old are they?"

"Vanya," Adesh snapped. "Don't condone this relationship."

Despite his love for them, Ali would never let family woes deter him from his blossoming relationship with Joy.

"I don't need your permission," Ali said in a controlled voice. "But I do want you to know how serious this relationship is. Joy is very special to me—and she won't be going anywhere. Despite your individual opinions on the matter."

Adesh went to speak up again, but Ali switched to Hindi and lit into them to such a point that when he was done, there were no more biting remarks, and both of his sons looked duly chastised.

"Money has nothing to do with it," Ali finished, answering his son's initial question.

"Try doing without it," Adesh countered, grinning.

"You first," Ali shot back, quirking a brow. "When have you made your own? Looks like I need to pull back on that easy stream of money going from my businesses into your account. Let you start from the bottom up."

Adesh nearly dropped the glass ornament as his back straightened. "You wouldn't dare. Grandpa would disown you, even more than he already has."

"Not if I'm trying to prove a point," Ali countered, lacing his hands and resting them on the glass desk. "People have a different appreciation when they're making it, not taking it."

Though Adesh grimaced as though he wanted to say more, he quickly simmered down. "Point taken."

"And another point you fail to realize," Ali said as the chef came in to serve an array of East Indian desserts. "Is that the millions I've made have nothing to do with your grandfather."

Adesh flinched. "But he said—"

"He lied." Ali studied his son. "All these years, you've been currying favor with him, and he's not the one with a successful business to his name. You backed the wrong horse, and you let him use you and try to jeopardize my business. You'll have to answer for that."

"But she's … Black," Nikhil said, frowning. "She's pretty and all that, but even your parents aren't going to like her."

"Which also gives *you* license not to like her," Ali said over the rim of his glass of Southern Comfort, the first adult drink he'd had on American soil and the one he indulged in at the beginning or the end of a successful venture. "Never realized how close-minded you were."

"No, just realistic," Adesh said, looking to his brother who nodded. "I mean, I've tapped into a chocolate honey before, and they are hot." His smile widened as though the memories were sweeter than he could voice, then his gaze leveled on Ali. "But even I know what side of the bed to keep them on."

"You are treading dangerously close to being on the wrong side of my anger," Ali replied. "I fulfilled my duty to the family name, and to each of my children. Now I can choose the woman I desire."

"I'd like to meet her," Adesh said, glaring at his father.

"Yes, if she's going to be important in your life," Vanya said, coming to her brother's side. "We'd like to approve."

Ali stood and went to the window to stand next to his daughter. "My relationships don't require your approval or anyone else's."

That statement was met with cold silence.

Adesh leaned back in his seat, narrowing his gaze at Ali. "So, it's a relationship, huh?"

"Indeed," Ali replied, taking a bite of Rasmulai. "One I cherish."

Nikhil perched on the edge of the dining table. "Well, at least she won't try to trap you with a kid."

"She's raising her niece and nephew," Ali said, chuckling inwardly. "She will still want children of her own at some point. And I'm all for obliging."

The four of them exchanged panicked and confused glances. Ali took in the somber expressions of his children, realizing that he'd given too much over to his wife's family and not enough attention to balance them, all because the family had more say in his former marriage and child-rearing than needed. He would rectify that in short order.

"Well, we're not—"

"Enough," Ali said, giving a pointed look at each one of them. "My life. My rules. My woman. Accept it or don't. It's not going to change how I live my life."

CHAPTER 13

*A*desh paced the rich, burgundy brocade rug that adorned the floor behind his desk.

"Brother, calm down." Nikhil said. "This is just a passing phase between Papa and the American."

"How dare he shame me in front of the family?" He raged, sweeping the files from his desk onto the floor. "He is putting a woman, a Black one, before family. It's unheard of. It's sacrilege. What is wrong with our women that he keeps binding himself to every piece of Black honey that he encounters? First that other one … Reign, now this one. What does she know of our culture? "

"She will learn and besides, Papa just wants to be happy. Who are we to begrudge him that? We owe our every happiness to him." Nikhil straightened his tie and reached for a mug of chai tea.

"Spoken like a mewling child at the golden teat. You just don't want him to cut you off from his money," Adesh said smoothing down his own tie. "Well, I don't need him or his chump change. I have my own. If he's not careful, I will take the company right from under his nose. Then we will see how well he does with the Black woman and her leechlike children.

"Adesh you don't know anything about …:"

41

He plucked a file from the floor and held it out.

"What is this?" Nikhil asked while thumbing through the folder. Surveillance photos spilled into his lap. He picked one up and squinted. "You had the woman followed?"

"She's a danger to us," Adesh countered, his voice raising an octave. "If she links me to any of my connects in the states it could ruin us,"

"What us? I just introduced you to some people at a party in New York. You were the one who started networking. If anyone is on the chopping block, it's you."

Adesh perched on the desk's edge and observed his younger sibling. Nikhil was not the smartest man in any room., But his charisma unlocked more opportunities than Adesh could ever do on his own. People feared Adesh because he had an edge that made people shy away. But not Joy, for some reason she seemed to look right through him.

All it would take was for Joy to turn her head and focus on the wrong things. He'd been great at building his shadow company under everyone's nose. But with the new woman taking up more and more time with his father, she was bound to snoop in their business affairs. Especially in her line of business.

"You realize this woman is a DEA Agent." Nikhul said while flipping through the photos.

"I do, but I have a remedy for that. She wears her heart on her sleeve. She's so wrapped up in Human Trafficking and her children and this new relationship she's trying to build with Papa, that there's no room for anything else. So long as she stays in her lane. We don't have a problem."

"She's not a stupid woman," Nikhil countered, flicking a gaze at one of the photos. "And as much as you'd like to think she's not paying attention. She is. She has to. No woman worth her salt would bring a strange man to her bed without him meeting her children first."

Adesh feared that very thing. "Then we remove her.

"We are not killing anyone."

"That's not what I meant," Adesh said, giving him a wide smile. "But it's interesting to hear you speak of it. It occurred to me that an unfortunate accident might pave the way for another leg of my venture," he said while thumbing through a small stack of mail. "Joy's mother is a vile thing. But with enough money she could be a useful tool. And then there is the Damien to consider. That drug dealer strikes me as an entrepreneur. If we can't get to her using logic, we'll get to her using love. Yes, I think Damien will do just fine."

Nikhil shook his head, all color drained from his skin. "You've gone mad. I am sure of it."

"Hardly. I'm a businessman, looking for avenues to build new venture. It's what we do. It's necessary to pay the help, even if it's an unsightly task."

"Papa will disown you for sure," Nikhil warned as he closed the file and placed it on the edge of the desk.

"Let him." He shrugged as if the consequences didn't matter as much as it should. "In another month or two I will be a billionaire on my own."

"You have given yourself over to Nakara," he said, using the Hindu name for Hell. "That is no place for you brother."

He watched his brother's gaze wither in sadness, causing his own smile to fade. Placing a hand on the younger man's shoulder. "This is the only place that feels like home to me."

CHAPTER 14

Joy had always wanted to take a trip on the Starlite Amtrak Train from California to Seattle. The fact that Ali had put things in place to make it happen in style warmed her heart. Their flight to LA was filled with conversations about the best parts of their careers and families. Joy checked in a few times to find that Jason was fine, and Lyric had actually stayed put with Ernie and Donna. Joy finally allowed her misgivings and concerns to subside and focused on enjoying her time with Ali.

They walked through the corridors of the Los Angeles train station, past the ticket offices to the elevators to the upper level which landed them in the Metropolitan Club.

"Aren't you glad that I'm a cheap date?" Joy teased.

"Just because you preferred to have an inexpensive and very unusual breakfast," he said after finishing a bite of pretzel dog. "doesn't mean you're cheap."

"I was only joking."

"I know," he said, chuckling. "These still aren't better than a Chicago Dog."

She held her hot dog out, saying, "True. True" and Ali tapped his to hers as if they were toasting to a good time.

Boarding time was in two hours, so they waited in the private club that was a perk of business class and sleeper car travelers. Ali had purchased two business class seats situated near the dining car, right above the cantina for casual dining, and just a car over from the sky deck.

"Why this particular train?" Ali asked, as they pulled out from the station.

"When I was younger, Ernie and Donna would take me on the Metra," she replied, settling into the comfortable leather chair in the nearly empty business class. "We'd ride the regular lines sometimes, but these trains were different. Wider and more comfortable seats, quiet conversations, the movement of the train was … comforting. So different from the CTA, public transport." She glanced out the window taking in the beauty of the ocean waves. "No music blaring or folks trying to sell me CDs, batteries, items boosted from different stores. No children wailing or having to hold my book bag close to me because it could walk off without me. The Metra passengers were working people, resting, planning their day, sleeping, reading. The difference mirrored my life. Ella's house was like the CTA, and the new life that I had in the building with people who actually loved me was like the Metra." She gave him a wide smile. "I was on the internet and saw an advertisement for this train, and it seemed like the ultimate ride."

The call for the train made the mass of people grab their items and head out to board. The windows on the ceiling skydeck curved into the framework, allowing perfect views of the scenery views changed from sandy beaches and oceans to woodsy plains covered by green grass, mountains, cows grazing, horses galloping in the open terrain, to snow-covered evergreens so tall they touched the clouds. She had wanted this trip at least once—but time never permitted. Always the children or something with the job. Never time for her to do what she wanted.

Joy laced her hand with his. "Thank you for this. And thank you for not assuming that I was ready for …"

"When it's time, it will happen, and it will be something amazing."

"No shortness of confidence on that, huh?"

"None at all." Ali pressed a kiss to the back of her hand. "There are some women you can tell will have the most pleasurable experience … if you take care of their needs first."

"Is that right?" she teased, giving him an ear to ear smile. "How do you know that about me?"

"Knew that you were a sensual creature the moment I laid eyes on you. Confirmed it when I held you."

Joy averted her gaze. "You frighten me."

"How so?"

"Even then, that first time made me feel …" she shrugged. "I can't even describe it."

Her eyes became glassy, but the tears would not fall. Ali cradled her against his chest. Only then did she relax, waiting for him to speak those unwanted platitudes. They never came. He must have perceived that those wouldn't work for Joy.

"So, what's the deal with your ex?"

"We were—are—friends. We share four children so we will always have a friendship. I'm happy that she's marrying the man she's always loved." Ali settled in, laid his head on her breasts. "The relationship with Reign opened me up for even better possibilities, to release my family's expectations and create some of my own. To find the woman who is the actual manifestation of what love truly is."

Joy stroked a hand through his hair. "You are so serious it's frightening. Is there any aspect of you that isn't intense?"

"I don't know any other way to be," he said. "I will not hurt you."

"Not intentionally."

She looked at him, watching his expressions transform from confusion to resigned understanding

The understanding touched her.

"My mother knew everything that was going on in her house, and let it go on until I became so sick that a neighbor took me to the hospital." She looked out to the ocean, so close to the moving train that with three good steps they could touch the water. "They arrested someone—but Ella claimed she was unaware and no one paid for that crime. That's the ugliness that I come from."

"But it's not who you are." He sat up so he could look her directly in the eyes. "You've spent so many years pushing the horrible feelings away that you're against letting any good ones in. Does anything about me say that I would hurt you?"

"Everyone has the potential to hurt someone."

"But they also have that same potential to love them," he countered, stroking a hand down her cheek. She settled into his arms and thought those words over for a long while. He extracted an iPad from a backpack under the seat.

"I notice you brought books with you on the trip."

"There's only so much scenery we can take in," he said. "I thought we'd indulge in a few literary endeavors."

Joy peered at the screen, checking out his electronic library. "You don't even know what I like to read."

"Sure I do. Jason sent me a list. Erotica," he said grinning. "Multicultural fiction. Contemporary fiction. Sci-Fi."

Joy frowned. "Those don't seem to be something you'd read."

"Not normally, but your son said the way to your heart wasn't candy or flowers, it was to turn the page."

She laughed. "You're going to read to me?"

"Of course. I figure we can choose the books by the opening line," he said, firing up his iPad. "That's classic. To me, books hook with that first line, that first paragraph, that first page, that first chapter—and it goes from there.

Joy snuggled into him. "I like it. Let's go."

Ali tapped the screen, opened the e-book application and scrolled, then said, "I cut him until I felt better."

Joy smirked and nodded. "Now that has my attention."

CHAPTER 15

Seattle
37 hours later
The Edgewater, Noble House Hotel

ALI'S TOUCH was a silken web of pleasure that spiraled to the heavens and back again. His hands trailed a fiery path from her shoulders, her breasts, her belly before he kissed the soft curve of her shoulder. He took her nipple in the heat of his mouth, drawing the sensations that rippled through her like the sweltering rain of desire that ended with a thundering release.

Ali was inside her again, the fullness of him so powerful that the world and all her problems ceased to exist; as did her ability to take a solid breath.

"Inhale, my love," he whispered, moving within her. "And let it out slowly."

Joy struggled to comply as he focused on her eyes. "Breathe. Just breathe."

Something was so right about him, about her being with him this way. None of the memories of her past came back to haunt her. She was in this safe place. The only scent was him. The only feel was him. The only sound was him. The only thing that mattered was … him.

The tears. Why tears when this was so close to heaven? But they came now, in this place, with Ali within her. They blinded her to the beauty of the man who trailed kisses across the soft skin of her breasts. Then took those kisses on a journey, where he savored her inch by inch, awakening and finding that which had been hidden— freedom to allow herself to be lost in the pleasure that had been out of her reach for far too long.

She reached for him, holding on to him, connecting them again, wanting him to fill that space inside, to ease the ache of belonging, the erase the absence of being loved this way. A thin layer of perspiration provided a silky slipperiness that warmed her. The sensations—pleasure, then slight pain sending more confusing signals to her body— which to enjoy, which to embrace, which to savor.

Joy tensed with every thrust, taking in the fullness of him, then flowered around him, her walls milking every inch, thirsty for the kind of nourishment that she'd been denied.

Her hand stroked the taut skin of his buttocks, then gripped them, pulled him into her as she rose to meet his next thrust, allowing the deep strokes of that ageless dance to guide her way.

Joy's first time. Those memories were locked in a place she could not open. She closed her eyes, praying that these new memories, the ones mastered by Ali, would sweep away the cobwebs of pain that she didn't realize existed.

"I love you," he whispered. "I love … you."

Yes, he did.

Joy believed him to the furthermost reaches of her soul.

Despite every effort to the contrary, she would love him, too.

CHAPTER 16

The call Joy feared would come arrived the moment they landed at O'Hare Airport. She turned on her cell and immediately, five messages came through from Jason, three from Ernie and one from Donna.

With a cry of dismay, Joy turned to Ali. "You have to take me to my mother's house right now."

"What's going on?"

"My children are in trouble," she said in a voice weighted with fear.

Frantic, Joy scrolled through all of the texts and pieced together that drug dealers had sprayed Ella's house with bullets. They were searching for Ebbie, who in a last-ditch effort to save herself, thought offering Lyric to Damien, a drug dealer who covered a large stretch of territory on the South side, to pay off her debt and make things square. Jason went to Ella's place trying to make sure that didn't happen. Now both of them were in trouble.

"We need to stop by my house and get my gun."

"I already have one," Ali confessed, wheeling the car into the fast lane past a grandmother barely hitting the speed limit. "It's in the glove compartment."

"Wait ... what? Why do you—"

"In my line of business people assume that I carry drugs on me. They are wrong, and some have to find out the hard way."

Ali placed a hand over hers, but he still managed to smoothly control the car at just over ninety. "Breathe my love. I know you're worried, but you won't do them any good if you fall apart right now."

She nodded. Ali was right. They were her top priority. She tightened her grip on his hand. Joy retrieved her cell to touch base with one of her co-workers, making sure the DEA had nearby agents on standby. She was all too aware that sometimes law enforcement made things worse. She'd promised to get in, assess the situation, then make contact if she needed backup.

When they arrived at Ella's house, it was pandemonium. The Garfield family was there en masse; armed with guns and handmade weapons she remembered from childhood. Each one of them had taught her how to protect herself so she'd never be vulnerable. No one could've known then that Joy's weak spots would be the kids she'd been strong-armed into raising. Damien's thugs had fanned out, weapons at the ready, but they were placed in check by the Garfield family. No one was making a move either way.

Damien emerged from the crowd and snatched Lyric. She screamed and fought as he tried to haul her to an SUV waiting at the curb.

"Stop," both Joy and Ali yelled simultaneously.

Ali drew his gun, training it on Damien. Some of Damien's thugs turned their weapons on Ali.

Neighbors had filed out of their houses and the apartment buildings to see what the commotion was all about but stayed at a safe distance. A few of them whipped out their cells, but Damien's henchmen brandished weapons, effectively putting a stop to anyone wanting to film the altercation.

"The girl stays here. I'll get you your money," Ali said, inching forward, keeping his gun on Damien. The criminal held Lyric in front of him, arms wrapped about her as if he had become her long-lost lover.

"How do I know I can trust you?"

"You have my word," Ali promised.

"Nigga, I don't know you or your word," Damien shot back, tightening his grip on Lyric's waist.

"No, you don't," Ali countered. "But what you should know is that there's no way you're leaving with Joy's children."

"That bougie bitch?" He glared at Joy and missed that Ali was still advancing. "Think she too good for e'rebody. Trying to be all white an' shit." He nodded as his gaze flickered between Joy and Lyric. "Nah. She gon' pay for a whole lotta sins. My grandma and lil' sis died because of her trifling ass."

"I was twelve," Joy screamed at him. "That wasn't my fault. You have Ella to blame for that."

Ella threw up her hands. "Naw, don put me in—"

"Don't you dare try to deny anything," Joy snapped at her mother, knowing full well she had everything to do with the woman and her child who were killed in that fire. All because the woman had dared to sneak Joy to the hospital after a tragic occurrence that she still couldn't remember.

"Yeah, well, putting her seed to work is payback," Damien said, grinning. "She's coming with us. Gon' bring in a lotta cash—after I have a taste." He turned to Jason. "Little man, too."

Damien's henchman grabbed Jason and backed away in the direction of yet another car with tinted windows before anyone could protest. "Some time on the corners will get him straight. Ebbie said the girl pays what she owe me. But we'll take him too. Need some new soldiers."

"Not happening. Send Lyric over here. Now," Ali said, lifting his gun directly in line with the man's forehead. "Release Jason."

"And who's gonna stop me?" Damien taunted. "We been out here all this time and ain't nobody call the police. And I ain't scared of you."

Ali lowered his gun, sending a bullet slicing right into the edge of the man's sneaker, then quickly repositioning it for his head again. The Garfield family put their weapons on the members of Damien's crew who were nearby, but not close enough to Lyric or Jason to do them harm. "The next one won't miss," Ali said through his teeth. "Let. Her. Go."

Ernie moved to Ali's side. Damien's men and the Garfield family each had someone in their sights. If things didn't get resolved soon, there would be a bloodbath.

Decision made, Ali's gaze connected with Lyric's, then to Jason. He gave a subtle turn of his head to his left. Lyric gave a subtle return nod, and so did Jason.

Watching the exchange, Joy inhaled to keep from crying out and telegraphing the next moves.

In the time it took to blink, Ali sprinted the rest of the distance between him and the man holding Lyric.

Lyric reached back, grabbed Damien in the groin and squeezed as hard as she could. He screamed in shocked pain as she threw her head back and it collided with his chin.

The impact threw them both off balance. She fell to the ground and rolled away from her captor.

Damien was still writhing on the ground as Ali jumped on him and pummeled him with his fist.

The man holding Jason was torn between helping his boss and keeping Jason restrained. His indecision cost him. Jason attempted to wrench free while Ernie lifted the shotgun and fired. The man relinquished his hold on Jason and fell to the ground, gripping his knees. A third man rushed forward toward Ali. Donna fired, leaving a hole where his heart should've been. The man pitched forward and crashed to the pavement with a thud mere inches from Ali's feet.

The Garfield family sprang into action, and soon Ella and Ebbie and the rest of Damien's men were taken down. During the chaos, Joy gathered up her children, while placing the call to request backup.

<h1 style="text-align:center">CHAPTER 17</h1>

"*P*apa, let me explain."

"No, my son," Ali said brushing Adesh's hand off his arm. "Your actions no longer match your words. You are not the man I thought you were."

"I was just trying to build an empire just like you."

"On the blood and bones of your fellow man?" Ali roared. "I never taught you to be so cruel. That man could have killed Joy's son and daughter."

"Damien wouldn't have taken it that far," Adesh countered, and his tone was more dismissive than apologetic.

"He had every intention of taking her daughter and defiling her. How would you feel if someone did the same to our beloved Kyra? She is the same age as joy's daughter. Would you be so cavalier if he held a gun to your sister's head?"

"But they are not her children. They did not come from her womb."

"They are from her heart. She put her life on hold to make sure that they had a better life. Just as I did with all of you," Ali said, gathering the key card and the company credit card from the desk. "Vanya

54

will take over the day-to-day operations. I have a better purpose for you."

CHAPTER 18

$\mathcal{A}$s they coasted to a stop in front of the hospital. Ali parked the car and removed his seatbelt. Adesh stared silently at his hands, fingers intertwined tightly.

"So you blame us? For making you a father?" Adesh asked, unable to meet his father's gaze.

Ali reached across the seat and hooked a finger under his son's chin and raised it so they eyes were level.

"You and your siblings have been my saving grace and my every happiness for years, but I am a man too, with thoughts and desires I can only share with the woman that I love. My love for you hasn't changed, but my heart is broken You have taken the brilliance you possess and perverted it. Come, t me show you your brilliance at work."

Ali wound his way through the hospital and past the nurse's station. He had already spoken to the director and explained his intent. They made it to a ward in the west wing and he opened a door to reveal a brightly painted room packed with hospital beds occupied by either catatonic patients or those who were screaming and thrashing while tied to the beds.

Adesh tried to back away from the scene but Ali shoved him

forward. "I have a new job for you. You are now the manager of this part of the drug rehabilitation ward. You will administer the reversal agent that you created to each of these patients. And you will stay for as long as the process needs for it to take effect. You will face the families that your drugs have destroyed and explain to them how your love of money is the source of their grief. You said so yourself … you are the author of their misery and the cure.

Adesh scanned the room and couldn't keep the disgust from his facial expression. "You can't make me stay here. I have my own money."

"Saved in one of my bank accounts. I will use it to build facilities around the world to clean up what you have done. Each one you will visit so that you never forget what your greed brought into the world."

"You can't make me do this." Adesh said, in a panicked shriek. "Mother won't allow it."

Ali clapped him on the back to hold him in place while giving him a smile that was neither warm nor welcoming. "She was the one that came up with the idea. Didn't you"

Adesh turned to see his mother standing there wearing a bright red sari. Tears streamed down her face at a rapid pace. The disappointment was so profound that his knees buckled and he fell to the ground.

CHAPTER 19

*J*oy's Home
Hyde Park

THE NEXT MORNING, Joy stayed within Ali's embrace, drawing strength. "I should've prepared Lyric for this possibility. They hurt her worse than they ever hurt me. Look at her."

"She's going to be alright," Ali whispered from the threshold of Lyric's bedroom door. "We'll make sure of it."

Joy shook her head, placing her hand on his chest to put some space between them. "I don't want you exposed to all of this madness with my family."

Ali moved in, lifted her chin to look Joy directly in her eyes. "If I can't be here through times like this, what makes you think I deserve to be there during the great parts? I choose to be with you—no matter what."

She nodded. "You're going to make me break out in the ugly cry."

"There is no such thing," he said, taking her in his arms again. "Tears mean your eyes are having an orgasm. This time it's a good one."

Joy burst out laughing, as Ali intended.

"Mama?" came in a voice so soft she thought she was hearing things.

Joy was at Lyric's side in an instant. "Good morning, honey."

"You tried to tell me," Lyric croaked.

Joy stroked a hand through Lyric's hair. "It's alright."

"They didn't even pretend," she said, nearly biting on the words. "The minute I told them I was coming to live with them, that man … he tried to …"

Joy leaned in, stroking her face. "They won't hurt you again, I promise."

"I can come back?" she asked in a voice just above a whisper. "Even after all those ugly things I said?"

"Of course, you always have a place in my home. You're my daughter," Joy said, kissing her forehead

Lyric sobbed. Several minutes after she composed herself, she looked to Ali and said, "See, this"—sniffle—"is what"—sniffle—"an ugly cry looks like."

Ali touched Lyric's face. "Still beautiful to me."

She grinned. "You're just saying that because you want to get in my mother's pants."

"It's what's between her ears that's more important," he said, placing a hand on Joy's chest. "It's what's under here that holds the key."

"Her breasts?" Lyric giggled.

"My heart," Joy said, laughing. "My heart."

"Always that," Ali agreed, then said to Joy. "I'll send a company here to help pack your things."

"What? I don't get …" Joy tilted her head. "What are you talking about?"

"The men who took her can find out where you live," Ali explained. "I want all of you to be safe. If you stay with me, no one's going to be swinging by my house trying to get Lyric or Jason not to testify."

Reality slammed into Joy. She hadn't even thought of that. She dropped down into the chair near to the bed. "We can just stay at a hotel."

"Joy, I don't want any of you within their reach." Ali looked at her until she could feel her resolve dissipating.

"I don't want to be a burden to you," she said. "All this baggage."

"Never a burden, my love," Ali whispered. "Another challenge for us to get through and come out on the other side."

"I like this guy," Lyric said with a wide smile.

Ali gave her a smile of his own. "You're not so shabby yourself."

Jason walked in with a tray carrying a bucket of Harold's Chicken. Ali went to help him.

Lyric shifted her gaze to Joy. "Mama, I'm sorry."

Joy embraced her daughter. "No need to be. When I was your age—"

"You were already on your own. Grandpa Ernie told me about the day you showed up and how strong and determined you were. He told me all the things you did to keep us safe." Lyric looked away. "And then I go and do something so stupid."

"Let me tell you something," Ali said returning to their side. He took Lyric's hand. "Every choice leads us to a better choice, or at least to an understanding of things we don't want. The pain will go away. Hurt and betrayal will go away. Might take a while, but what will be left in its place is a strength and determination that will make you unstoppable." Ali reached for Joy's hand, then motioned for Jason to join them. "And we'll both be here to help you get to that point. If you let us."

"You'll be there for my mom, too?"

Ali's look was filled with an intense emotion as he said, "Most definitely."

Joy's heart took that final leap into love.

CHAPTER 20

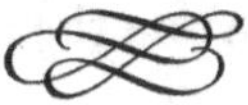

One month later, the Amtrak pulled out from Union Station heading toward a final destination of New Orleans. Three of Ali's children were seated near Jason and Lyric, entertaining them with stories about India and places that they traveled. Soon they would take a trip on the EuroRail that would cover places where none of them had been.

"What's the first word that came to mind when you first laid eyes on me?"

Ali shifted Joy in his arms, taking the time to choose between the truth and the version that wouldn't send her flying out of his arms. The answer was somewhere in between. "Lost," he whispered. "You seemed ... lost."

Joy didn't take her eyes off him as she said, "That's fair. What's the word that comes to mind when you think of me now?"

"Mine," he whispered. "All mine."

Joy couldn't help but smile.

Story notes **on *Loving All of Me* . . .**

. . .

My first Cuddle Party was an exhilarating experience. I held onto an article in the *Chicago Red Eye* for a year before I got up the courage to attend. The event taught people of all ethnic backgrounds and genders what it was to experience safe, non-sexual touch. No other books that I've read covered this event and with the valuable input of fellow national bestselling authors Lisa Watson and J. D. Mason, I thought I would share how two people could become deeply connected even when sex wasn't on the table.

If you enjoyed *Loving All of Me*, please leave a review. On the next pages, I offer a FREE BOOK download and also a few sneak peeks of other novels that you might enjoy.

"When did policemen start looking like *that*?" Elise Payne gasped, putting a tighter grip on the steering wheel.

She had been pulled over for speeding but she couldn't believe that someone as breathtaking as Officer Friendly had stepped out of the cruiser. The man had expressive, dark brown eyes and smooth golden features—a proud nose and sensuously curved lips—carved into a ruggedly handsome face that was damn pleasant to look at along with a muscular body that was nothing but pleasure to watch. Elise normally enjoyed milk chocolate, but maybe it was time to give vanilla bean some consideration.

The fact that this delay would probably make her miss the train slipped her mind as she became totally smitten by the most handsome male since Jesus turned water into wine. She could picture those gorgeous lips doing wicked, forbidden things to her—the kind of things that made a woman start speaking in tongues, the kind of things that made a woman leave religion at the altar and dive headfirst into temptation, skinny dip in an overdose of sin, and—

"License, insurance, and registration, ma'am."

Her fantasy circled the bowl and flushed right down the drain with those words. She let out a long, slow breath and said, "May I take my hands off the steering wheel?"

He nodded, grimacing as he did so.

Elise inched her hand into her satchel and produced a license, then leaned toward the glove compartment and froze at the thoughts whipping through her mind. *Registration, no problem. Insurance, huuuuge problem. Expired. Five hundred dollars.*

She tried to keep the despair from showing on her face as she slid the documents to him. Elise watched his every move as he snailed a walk back to his cruiser.

Seriously? Can't you go any faster?!

Several minutes ticked by before he returned. She quickly put her hands on the wheel before he made it all the way to the driver side window.

This time, he sighed with impatience. "It's safe to take your hands off the wheel, Ms. Payne. I'm a Burnham officer. It's the Chicago police who are trigger-happy."

Elise remained completely silent. Maybe if she zipped her lips, he would give her the ticket and let her be on her damn way.

"Do you realize you were going 77 in a 45?" he asked.

"Actually, I thought it was just 65, but 77 it is," she shot back.

He paused for a moment, his right eyebrow lifting. Elise saw a sudden slight uplift at the corners of his lips. There was a fullness that made them the most kissable pair she'd seen in a long time. What was it about this man's lips that invited her to give him a second and third look? What was it about those dark brown eyes that held a sparkle of mischief, but a smidgen of pain behind them? And how was that so easy for her to recognize?

"*Why* were you going so fast?" he asked.

"Because I was trying to catch that train *riiiiight* there," she replied, gesturing to the silver and orange commuter whizzing past them on a black bridge overhead. Her heart sank. All hopes of landing that new position were gone.

"There'll be another one coming along."

The train disappeared from their view, and she returned her focus to him. "Not in enough time to make it downtown for my first day." She slumped in the leather seat and whispered, "And this one had a chance to go permanent."

The officer looked down at her, as though summing things up, summing *her* up. "Well, I'm not going to ticket you for speeding."

Her grateful gaze locked on him.

"Or for the fact that you weren't wearing a seatbelt."

She opened her mouth to protest that she had only slipped it off because he had taken so long, but shut it and nodded her thanks.

"Or for the fact that your insurance expired last week."

"Thank you, Officer Montgomery," she murmured as he slid the items back to her. Their hands touched briefly, and a jolt of electricity whipped through her. She looked up in time to see his shocked expression. *Ah, he felt it too.*

At that moment, however, the only electricity she needed to worry about was ComEd. Her lights and power were about to become a distant memory if she didn't dance into their office with something more than a handful of "give me" and a mouthful of "much obliged."

"This picture," Officer Montgomery said, gesturing to a photo of her with her sister where they both wore black hats--derbies or Dobbs as her grandmother called them. The smiles were from a happier time when they went to a mystery dinner and played detective. They were the only ones to solve the murder that evening and were awarded those special hats by the event hosts. Strangely enough, her ex had been mean enough to take those with him, knowing how much they meant to her.

She explained this to the officer and a sadness came over those dark brown eyes before he tipped his hat. "So sorry to hear that. You have a nice day, ma'am. And leave a little earlier next time."

When he walked back to the cruiser, Elise laid her forehead on the steering wheel. Tears she had been holding back for months finally had their reign. The energy to forge on, to get up and dust herself had never abandoned her—but everything happening at once had finally taken its toll.

Elise moaned as the tears increased. Her entire life was at a standstill and most wasn't of her own making. All of her money was gone. Every single dime she had had been used to keep her twin sister alive, only to lose that beautiful soul to kidney and liver failure last month.

No sooner than she could breathe again without razor blades tearing into her lungs from that loss, did her rich ex-husband swoop down with a team of lawyers and manage to steal her baby boy while she was distracted with grief and the fallout of her family's displeasure at what she'd done to keep her sister alive as long as she could. Yet, she had gathered up whatever resources she could, fought with everything she had, only to lose her son anyway.

Another blow, another setback, another harsh, bitter loss. The last being the one which left her so out of sorts—at least financially. The fact that Ameritech's merger put her and 5,000 other people on the unemployment line was a wakeup call that blared in her ears every day.

Elise sniffled and blindly reached into her satchel for a tissue. She couldn't even drive downtown and park because what she had left in the bank had been shelled out to pay mortgage, a few groceries, and get a train pass to carry her through the month. She didn't complain because at some point, she'd catch her breath and a break—both at the same time.

Fighting for the life of her sister was something Elise would never regret. But the aftermath to her finances and the never-ending strain between her and the family was putting her closer to the edge of emotional bankruptcy.

A tap on the window startled her.

Elise absently patted her tears away with the tissue.

"Ma'am, is everything all right?" Officer Montgomery questioned.

She rolled down the window. "Your kindness was the nicest thing that's happened to me in a long time." She looked up toward the empty bridge. "Thank you. But the next train comes in two hours. By then, the agency will call someone else to take the spot I was going for."

The officer scanned the area. Only a few cars zipped by them. "Traffic isn't bad right now. You could make it downtown in about thirty minutes and still get there on time."

"I could but …" Elise hesitated then abruptly added, "I can' t …" She couldn't voice the words—she had everything, down to the last penny budgeted—and parking downtown was an arm, a leg and a couple of someone else's toes.

Officer Montgomery placed a hand over hers. "I'm really sorry."

His touch was wonderful. She centered her self-control with a quickness. "What's done is done. Recently my life has been hit with more curve balls than a dodge ball tournament. So I'm going home to regroup. I'll be fine." Her voice wavered on the last sentence, but she took a deep breath, tossed her hair over her shoulder, and held her head high. Seconds later, she turned the key in the ignition to start the car. "Take care."

Officer Montgomery reached for her hand again. "No, you're not," he ordered. "You will park your car in that lot just ahead. Then you'll get into my car and I'll get you to work on time." He stepped back and finished, "That's what you're going to do."

She looked at him, her tears blurring her vision. "That's what I'm going to do?"

He nodded.

Elise took a moment before whispering, "All right, then."

Officer Montgomery headed for his squad car again and added, "I'll be right behind you."

This time, she did smile ... a little.

Download on Amazon: https://bit.ly/StopinthenameofloveU

SUGAR AIN'T SO SWEET

I will die if I stay here ...

Shannon's entire family sat at the dinner table enjoying a meal which took her three hours to prepare, while she mowed the jungle of their front yard, seething the entire time. She stopped to empty the bag but froze when her mother-in-law's voice carried from the open pantry window, "I had to fake a damn heart attack to make this stupid heifer get with the program."

Faked a heart attack? Wait. What?

Monique Hallerin had faked that entire one-month ordeal so Shannan would take over the daunting task of shopping, preparing, cooking, then serving Sunday dinners for fifteen people every week, only to criticize nearly everything that Shannan did. Faked it so Shannan's husband, Zach, would pick up the slack on her bills. All while her brothers-in-law and most of her children parked their lazy behinds at the dining room table every Sunday and didn't lift a finger to help. Shannan was way past tired—exhausted was a better word.

"Guests don't wash dishes," her husband said when she mentioned they could pitch in with clean up. Well, to be honest, neither did he and he hadn't been a guest since they'd said, "I do."

What she should've said on the day they were married, fifteen years ago was, "I don't," then ran past his overbearing mother and four shiftless brothers then out the church doors to freedom.

"I had to fake a damn heart attack to make this stupid heifer get with the program."

Shannan, who had seven children of her own, was now responsible for duties that her mother-in-law had done for most of her non-married life; catering to those grown ass men sitting at her dining room table at this very moment while Shannan was outside doing something she had first asked her husband, then one of them, to do.

Rage hit Shannan full force.

She staggered away from the mower, rushed into the house, ran up the stairs and snatched up her tote. She halted at the threshold of her bedroom for a moment, extracting the small shoebox in the back of the closet. A set of credit cards, passport, birth certificate, social security card, and all the hidden cash found its way into the tote. She glanced at the summer wardrobe spilling over into Zach's side and decided there wasn't anything she wanted to take. She tipped down the rear stairway into the kitchen, snatched the keys from a hook near the door to put as much distance between herself and those people as possible.

Shannan only vaguely heard the youngest of her seven children call her name. Her heart constricted as she ignored them, tears blinding her as she slid behind the wheel of an SUV that was almost a second home. Basketball. Volleyball. Football. Gymnastics. PTA. Never any breaks between or any time for her to simply breathe.

I will die if I stay here.

Those seven words came to mind, summarizing her current status. Something that first hit her when she had the argument with Zach before his family arrived …

"No, my brothers shouldn't have to wash a dish in my house," Zachary had protested without bothering to look up from the current prosthetics project spread out over the basement. "My mother spent a week in the hospital and she can't handle it anymore. This dinner is how we stay close. I don't see what the problem is."

"The problem is, that it's all too much," she replied, putting aside her own work on the latest puzzle she was creating for the daily newspaper to focus more on the conversation that was long overdue. "I'm beginning to dread Sundays. I don't have any day of rest."

"Well, if you gave up that job you've been playing at then you wouldn't be so tired all the time," he quipped.

"I shouldn't have to give up anything," she shot back. He'd always considered the six figures she made from being a Master Cruciverbalist—crossword puzzle creator—frivolous. His career as a prosthetist brought in just under what she did. There had been a bone of contention on that score.

"Then it looks like you're going to be busy." Zachary shrugged. "You'll be alright."

"Wouldn't have to be so busy if you and the boys helped around here," she countered.

"My mother raised five boys on her own and never complained," he said, keeping his focus on the circuitry in his hands.

"And she was on her own because she ran your father off," she replied. "Let's be real about that."

Zachary's face twisted into a mask of annoyance as he glared at her. "I can't talk about this with you."

"I'm done talking. I'm tired," she snapped. "There's going to come a time when I say to hell with it."

Zach paused at the end of the wooden bench, scoffing as he asked, "And where are you going to go? Who's going to be a father to seven children?"

"They have a father," she said, and the sorrow of her reality was heavy indeed. "I need a husband."

The moment Shannan hit the expressway, she wiped her tears with the back of a trembling hand. A startling thought hit her. She could not leave her baby girl in that house.

Download it on Amazon: https://bit.ly/SugaraintsosweetU

10 DAYS OF PLEASURE

Shadow Bay, Maryland 9pm

"The chatty ones get on my nerves man. Only way to shut them up is to feed them or—"

Dallas toweled his head before sitting down on the bench. Taking part in tournaments where the ticket sales and other proceeds went to charity kept his mind occupied, but little else. The seconds bled by leaving his mind to build frightening images of Alicia being anywhere but beside him.

"Man are you even listening to me?" His raven-haired friend asked. "You've been cagey as hell all weekend. Did she call or leave a text?"

"Alicia is about her business." Dallas replied pulling the phone from the top shelf of his locker. He mashed a thumb against the thumbprint scan and frowned. "Last thing she needs is some clingy man dogging her steps from here to the bathroom."

A text would have sufficed. Hearing her voice would have eased the strange pain blossoming in his chest. Did she need anything? Had someone made her smile that day? Did she miss him? The questions rolled through him in sickening waves. Being the source of all those things and more occupied more of his headspace every day. At night, his prayer life was filled with her name.

He had to smile at himself. His career took off and the closest he ever made it to a church was on CME: Christmas, Mother's Day, and Easter Sunday. From the moment he met Alicia Mitchell, the prayer life he tucked neatly away had crackled and hummed like a live wire. He'd never admit it in front of his teammates, but while they were off celebrating, sometimes he begged off just to spend hours talking to her on the phone or pouring over the old black leatherbound bible that belonged to his grandfather.

If you ever want to find your dream girl, son. All you have to do is look in the Good Book. Read Proverbs 31.

From the moment Dallas took her hand and pressed a kiss to the back of it, the stars lined up and danced. Alicia was his first thought in the morning and the last one at night. Sure, he had his choice of the most beautiful women in the world jockeying for the prime real estate at his side. Some were nice enough. Others flipped their extensions and fluttered their butterfly wing eyelashes and asked where the next awards dinner was happening but cared nothing about his day.

Alicia asked, each question formed by her beautiful mouth flowed through him like music and felt like cool water on parched land. She cared if he had eaten and how practice went. And when he talked about his games, Alicia was right there in the moment with him listening to the highs and lows.

Never once did he look over and see her scrolling through a cell phone or buffing her manicured nails on the sofa, biding her time before asking if they could go shopping or to some swanky restaurant where everybody who was anybody went to be seen.

Adrian Hernandez poked Dallas in the arm breaking his train of thought. He glanced at his longtime friend in sports and life. "Sorry. What were you saying?" Dallas asked returning the phone to the shelf.

"Damn, her powers of persuasion that thick? I've been talking to you this whole time and other than an occasional grunt all I get is radio silence. You used to rattle on about how you hated clingy women. You should be happy she's not blowing your phone up," Hernandez said as he swiped some deodorant under one arm and then the other.

"Alicia is different."

From her hazel eyes to an hourglass shape with a few extra minutes for good measure, Alicia was perfect. She wasn't rail thin with cosmetic surgery to overcompensate for anything. And then there was her intelligence and wit. He could sit and listen to her for hours discussing something she heard or read in the news.

Hernandez paused and shook his head. "They all are, but when the relationship goes south, they take it out on the next man they hook up with or make you pay through the nose to get rid of them. Like a severance package or settlement for services rendered."

Dallas pulled on a shirt and worked at his belt buckle then shrugged. He'd seen his share of women with that hungry look on their faces when they believed that a one-night stand would turn into something more. Few marriages ever survived the rigors of fame. They were the worst to witness. A woman who put her career on hold to support her husband's dreams only to be replaced with a newer younger model.

Walking through the gauntlet of reporters and fans, Dallas could always spot the women blinded by the lights, cameras, and parties that never ended. Until they did. Some moved on and hooked up with the next available athlete. Others stood behind the barriers cradling children silenced with child support payments, or worse, simply ignored as his teammates moved on to their way to the next party or game.

Dallas glanced at his friend presently working the wedding band off his finger and thought of Alicia. She never said she'd been hurt or marginalized in a relationship, and he didn't dare to ask for fear that it would trigger a painful memory, but the signs were there. Sometimes he'd catch her looking off at something in the distance and the pain would well in her eyes. Her countenance would change, and the storm clouds would form and just as the threat of a hard rain became imminent, Alicia would take in a deep breath and smile.

"Alicia's been hurt pretty badly, but it didn't make her bitter. If anything, it made her better. She doesn't need a man to validate her. She made her own way in the world and—" Dallas said before pausing to gather his thoughts. "She has her own life and her own interests. If there's a man in the picture it's a privilege. Not a necessity."

Hernandez whistled. "She got to be something else if you're looking in her direction. All the pretty women standing on the sidelines want to kiss your ring and other things," he said wriggling his eyebrows.

None of them compared to Alicia. The confidence and intelligence rose from her like heat. The way she walked and talked, the woman had more grace and style than all the groupies in his orbit. Alicia didn't need, to glue a man's elbow to her chest. Her validation and her self-worth weren't tied up in the man standing beside her. She wasn't built to walk behind a man. Alicia would walk beside him or walk alone. Either way she would make the journey. He just wanted to be the man privileged enough to accompany her on along the way.

Dallas put the last of his belongings in the sports bag and closed the locker. Scanning the room, he smiled. The Cygnet Sports

Complex in Shadow Bay, Maryland had one of the nicest no frills locker rooms he and his team ever visited. Most locker rooms looked like a Sports Medical facility. The massage tables and deep hot tubs were glorious, but there were days when Dallas longed for the simplicity of a high school locker room.

One college ball championship landed him at The Dance. Four pro basketball championship rings later, and an MVP trophy propelled him into the stratosphere. The fanfare grew old and where Hernandez still basked in the adoration, Dallas missed the quiet things. Family dinners and walks on the beach with Walter, his old British bulldog. He missed going to a florist shop to pick out just the right flowers and talks about music and classic movies or television. Sportscasters nick-named Dallas 'The Machine' because he was unstoppable. Now all he wanted was to be human, to be seen, to be... loved.

Alicia gave him that. Within the last few weeks, the shy meek woman had upended his world, kicked out the crudely constructed props he fashioned out of ego and filled his life with meaning and purpose beyond the floorboards.

He glanced at the platinum diver's watch on his wrist. Twelve hours away from her made the pieces of his soul shift around inside like broken glass. Forget mortar or glue. Alicia was the quicksilver moving through his bloodstream and the gold seam fusing his humble beginnings to a future that had no boundaries. With her, the world was new. Without her even the air seemed thinner, lacking substance and that wicked elixir called life.

"Must be some kind of miracle worker in reserve."

"What?"

Hernandez rolled his eyes and pointed at the phone jittering in Dallas' hand. Alicia's name scrolled across the screen, and he nearly dropped the phone.

"Goodbyes just hurt, and hello is too small a word," Alicia said, her voice just barely above a whisper.

Dallas walked over to the full-length mirror and searched his own eyes. Maybe it was the slow intoxicating register of her voice or the way her tongue caressed the Ls in the word hello. If the ache in his throat were any indication, eleven hours, and thirty-seven minutes away from Alicia Mitchell was more than he could stand.

"There's an old poet that talks about seeing the world in a grain of sand and eternity in an hour."

"Never would have figured you for a William Blake guy." She purred. Immediately his mind filled with the image of her bare shoulder slipping into view. The memory of the champagne-colored satin robe flowing over her silky skin made his mouth go dry.

"Oh, I am a man of many talents and interests. I can't wait to share them all with you—" Dallas bit down on the last of his statement and laughed, "Didn't mean it like that."

"Sad, was looking forward to learning all about your talents," A slow sexy moan slid from her throat. Every word was soaked in white hot ecstasy.

"You sound like Christmas over there."

The cramp of desire just below his belt buckle made it difficult to stand up straight. Dallas put a hand on the cold metal frame of the mirror. Visions of a sunset and Alicia dressed in nothing but her smile wreaked havoc on his resolve.

"Where are you, babe?" he asked willing himself back into some semblance of control.

"Heading to Scotland."

His heart slammed against his chest. "Wait what? Scotland?"

LOVING ME FOR ME

"With all of those degrees," Devesh Maharaj countered. "I'm sure you're very much aware of the numbers. Black women outnumber Black men nearly three to one. More if you count the ones who are not available to them—married, in jail, gay, or those who don't want to commit to marriage."

The audience clapped, the more enthusiastic applause coming from Black women.

"They'll go to their graves while waiting for the Black man who God's supposed to mysteriously recycle so she can have her turn," Devesh said. "He took two fish and five loaves of bread, and it became enough to feed a multitude. But I never heard of Him using His power of multiplication to create extra brothers when there are already so many other desirable seeds. Those seeds on the ground might at least bloom into a relationship that is more than a placeholder until a good Black man mysteriously comes along. And it might be the best thing that's ever happened for both of them."

This time the audience whooped, hollered, and laughed and Sharon placed an encouraging hand on his shoulder. Sheryl nodded and had an ear-splitting smile.

Shawn's face darkened with anger. "So now you speak for Black women?"

"I don't have to speak for Black women because I only have to focus on one woman." He took a sip from the coffee mug and returned it on the coaster. "A woman I love, a woman whose spirit I'm not going to crush just to satisfy my ego. You have a wife—she's your business. I have my wife—she's my business. I'm not all up in your finances. I'm not all up in your bedroom." From the corner of his eye, Devesh saw Sheryl and Sara nodding and putting the evil eye on Shawn. "Your ego took pleasure in hurting Reign. I take pleasure in helping my woman to heal."

"My woman?" Shawn examined Reign before looking back to Devesh. "Sounds like some cave man white boy mess."

"Number one, I'm not White, I'm East Indian. And my second point is too many men have used the word wife in a way that implies property. Saying my woman is primal, instinctual." Devesh's smile disappeared as his eyes narrowed to slits when they focused on Shawn. "It means I will nail someone's balls to the wall if they come at her the wrong way."

"Are you threatening me? On live television?" Shawn said, shoulders stiffening.

"Not threatening anyone. I'm going to need you to keep my woman's name out of your mouth." Devesh leaned in, causing Shawn to slide back. "See, you're not upset about the most important part of the equation. You're upset about the money. If I wasn't rolling in it right now, you wouldn't blink about who I chose as my mate." Devesh wagged a finger in Shawn's direction. "So my brother, you're going to have to stay mad—I mean the next seventy years worth of mad, because I'm going to be loving my woman until there's no more love to be had."

Download it on Amazon: https://bit.ly/LovingMeForMeU2

KING OF DURABIA

"You risked your life for my grandson," Sheikh Aayan said, his voice echoing through the ornate throne room. "Ask for anything and I will see what can be done."

Ellena scanned the expectant faces of the throngs of people who had gathered for this unexpected audience with the ruler of Durabia. Most of their tunics and dishdashas differed from her casual attire of a simple white blouse and black slacks. "Thank you, but that isn't necessary. I did what anyone would do."

"Evidently, not everyone," he said, and his angry glare focused on the bodyguard, caregivers, and everyone who had stood by when Javed, the little royal, had swept past Ellena and landed on the moving conveyor belt.

All of them had frozen in place the moment Javed brushed against the rubber bounding strip and was sucked into the void. The video of

Ellena dropping her tote bag, diving in after him, and cradling him in her arms as they were both tossed through the maze of steel and vinyl, all while being battered by suitcases and duffel bags alike, went viral.

Ellena had closed her eyes, bracing under each blow. Javed's laughter was a stark contrast to her pain. The cameras caught everything, including the tail end of the journey when Ellena tumbled out of the final drop onto another belt and finally into the metal cart that would carry the luggage onto the plane. Security finally found their legs and scrambled to make it to Ellena and the little boy before they sustained further injuries. Well, before she did. Her fleshy body was all the protection that Javed needed.

Javed Khan, a great grandson of the Royal Family, was completely unharmed. Ellena, on the day of arrival for a class reunion vacation, had to be rushed to the hospital. They kept her overnight. She sustained a few cuts and bruises that matched the dent in her ego when the entire world saw her tossed head over ass multiple times. And when the adrenaline wore off and the fear kicked in, the little royal refused to let her go. He even had to travel in the emergency transport with her because none of the guards or caregivers managed to force him to release his hold on Ellena.

Now she stood in a palace situated in the heart of a metropolis in the Middle East with a décor that was unrivaled by anything she'd ever seen. Gold—everything was layered with it—the walls, doors, accented by purples and reds that added a sultry warmth to all of the opulence of the furniture, paintings, and draperies covering massive windows.

"Well, to be honest, I haven't wanted much," she said with a nervous laugh. "And the only thing I don't have is a husband. But I'd love to have a place here in Durabia, where I can come and go as I please. If that is at all possible."

"Done," the Sheikh said, beckoning to the man who had visited the hospital twice to see about her condition. "Kamran, come."

"Wait. What?" She laughed and rested a hand on her ample bosom. "An apartment, really?"

"Your new husband," he answered with a grand gesture that would have made Vanna White proud. "This is my oldest son."

The man was drop-dead gorgeous. Olive complexion, dark hair, goatee neatly trimmed to perfection, and piercing brown eyes that missed nothing. He was more suited to a fashion runway than a palace. Truthfully, she wasn't sure if it was the tunics, neat beards, head coverings or what. Durabia seemed to have no shortage of handsome men. But the Sheikh's son was a masterpiece, exuding the kind of confidence that came with a man who was certain of his place in the world. His gaze swept across her face with a complexion slightly darker than his olive tone, then quickly covered the distance over her curves, then his lips lifted in a warm, appreciative smile that practically lit up his dark brown eyes and sent heat straight to places that had been dormant since the Queen of Sheba caused King Solomon to lose his entire mind.

Ellena shook her head, clearing her mind of all manner of wickedness that came after that wonderful assessment. "I think you misunderstood. I was joking about the husband part. The apartment, time share or whatever you call them here, that's all I really want."

"You will have both," the Sheikh commanded with a nod of finality no one would dare to question. "A husband and a place here. My son needs a wife and you mentioned you do not have a husband. Problem solved."

"But doesn't he have to give you heirs or something?" She instinctively brought her hands near her belly. "My eggs are old enough to be married and have children of their own by now."

First, a roar of laughter went up from him. A few moments later, it was mirrored by everyone standing around her. Yes, that line was funny, but the one thing she understood was the unfairness of the situation. At least for Kamran. And that was no laughing matter.

The Sheikh waved away that thought. "That will not be a concern. He is unable to give you or any woman children. And a woman of African descent will never sit on the Durabian throne. We are safe on that score."

A shadow of sadness flickered in Kamran's eyes and his skin

flushed a shade darker. Ellena tried to read a deeper meaning into his father's words. She still came up with *unfair*. "So, you just throw him to a random woman because he can't give you an heir? He is *still* a man. He *still* has value," she insisted. "A brain, intelligence, and a purpose." She inhaled, trying to tamp down on her anger. "The apartment is fine, Sheikh. Thank you, but I will not be foisted on a man who has no say in the matter. That's downright cruel."

A gasp came from the core of people around them before silence descended in the room. Even Kamran flinched.

The Sheikh's face darkened with anger as he slowly came to his feet. "Are you refusing—"

"Give me nine days—"

All eyes focused on the handsome man, who left his father's side and moseyed toward her like some type of Arabian cowboy. All swagger, no gun necessary.

"Give me nine days," he repeated and moved across the expensive Persian carpet until he stood in front of her, towering over her near six-foot height by three inches of his own. "Nine days for me to show you Durabia, to answer any questions you may have. To let you explore the place, the people, the culture. Then you decide."

Ellena found it hard to catch her breath. The man was so virile she felt warm all the way to her follicles. "Nine days? I have to go home. I have a job back there. I used all of my vacation and two of my sick days for this trip."

"Your job?" he asked, frowning as though he couldn't fathom what the word meant.

"Yes. A job. Nine to five. Benefits. All of that. You know, what regular folks do to keep an address."

Kamran remained silent for a few moments as he peered at her. "How much do they pay you?"

She winced, then flickered a gaze to his right and felt the intensity of everyone's attention. "It doesn't matter."

"How much?" He beckoned for her to come nearer. "Whisper it to me."

Ellena hesitated a moment, then complied, moving so close she inhaled the intoxicating scent of sandalwood. She managed to whisper an answer, then inched back to put a little distance between them.

"For the rest of your life?" he asked, his tone and wide eyes reflecting the incredulity registered in his facial expression.

"Until I'm sixty-seven and retire," she replied, daunted by his tone. "But there's also health benefits and other factors that I can't put a number on."

Kamran blinked as though doing a set of mental calculations and coming up with what probably amounted to simple interest on his bank account. "Give me the particulars and I will wire the money into your account."

She parted her lips to protest but he held up a hand. "Saying yes to taking me as your husband is still your choice. With this, I am simply ensuring your peace of mind. And as a gift for your kindness, your selflessness in saving a child who was a stranger to you."

Ellena let out a long, slow breath, because staying here permanently, marrying him, would be a lost cause. She loved her job as a personal assistant at Vantage Point. Alejandro Reyes, a "Fixer" of everything from political and corporate espionage, to terrorist attacks, was the absolute best person to work for. And she loved the predictability of her life. Traveling overseas was the most adventurous event in her life. Still, curiosity won out over common sense and she said, "All right. Thank you."

"Now we go about the business of getting to know one another," he said, smiling as though her consent brought him much pleasure. Evidently, he wanted this to happen and the intensity of his gaze bore into her soul. "So that you can make an informed decision, yes?"

She glanced over his shoulder, taking in some of the envious looks a few of the women tried to hide. "Why are you doing this?" she asked him. "Why are you allowing them to serve you up to some foreign woman as if you do not have value?"

"Because I recognize this is God's will," he answered. "And who am I to leave a precious gift unwrapped?"

Her eyebrows drew in, as she tried to decipher the hidden

meaning behind his words. The man had a peaceful, confident air but also a playful vibe about him.

"Yes, that was a double entendre." His smile widened and she could swear the heavens opened up and smiled with him.

Good Lord, I'm in trouble.

Download it on Amazon: https://bit.ly/KingofDurabia1

ABOUT NALEIGHNA KAI

Naleighna Kai is the *USA TODAY, Essence®*, and national bestselling and award-winning author of several controversial women's fiction, contemporary fiction, Christian fiction, Romance, Suspense, and Science Fiction novels that plumb the depth of unique love triangles and women's issues. She is also a contributor to a New York Times bestseller, one of AALBC's 100 Top Authors, a member of the Chicago Vocational School Hall of Fame (CVS), Mercedes Benz Mentor Award Nominee, and the E. Lynn Harris Author of Distinction.

In addition to successfully cracking the code of landing a deal for herself and others with a major publishing house, she continues to "pay it forward" with the experience of NK Tribe Called Success, the Kings of the Castle Series, the Knights of the Castle Series, and by organizing the annual Cavalcade of Authors which gives readers intimate access to the most accomplished writing talent today. She resides in Chicago where she is working on her next two books.

ABOUT STEPHANIE M. FREEMAN

Stephanie M Freeman is a Hybrid author that began her professional writing career back in 2012 when Crimson Romance, an imprint of Simon & Schuster published her novel, *Necessary Evil*. Since then, she has explored different writing genres including, Mysteries, Thrillers, Romantic Suspense and the Paranormal. Stephanie is also a member of Naleighna Kai's Tribe Called Success and the Cavalcade of Authors.

She often jokes that with a shot glass or a cup of coffee in one hand, she is known for writing an erotic tale or two. Stephanie has amassed a loyal group of fans who eagerly await her latest releases. Her Diamonds, Blood and Shadows Series is a fan favorite. Her other books include: Unfinished Business, Nature of the Beast and A Letter from Yesay. Writing as Aracyne (Air Ruh Sin) Kelly, she also wrote: Peculiar Kindness and Heaven's Girl.

Stephanie is the host of the wildly popular Club House Event called Murder, Mayhem and Mysteries (and the people who love them). With multiple five-star reviews of her work, Stephanie M. Freeman continues to push literary boundaries.

Visit Stephanie on the Web:
Website: https://bit.ly/Stephaniemfreemanwebsite
Newsletter: https://bit.ly/stephaniemfreemannewsletter
Sociotap: http://bit.ly/StephMFreemanST